THE SECRET OF STORMVIEW

When Meg Warren loses her teaching job in London, she returns to Pendarren, the small Devonshire village where she grew up. The place still holds many memories for her. Some, like her childhood sweetheart, Adam Eden, are good. But others, such as her father's mysterious suicide, and Stormview, the sinister house just outside the village that is almost permanently shrouded in mist, have haunted her for years. When Meg takes on a job at Stormview as governess to the new owner's twin girls, she needs all her courage . . .

ROSEMARY SANSUM

THE SECRET OF STORMVIEW

Complete and Unabridged

LINFORD
Leicester

First published in Great Britain in 2017

First Linford Edition
published 2018

A catalogue record for this book is available
from the British Library.

ISBN 978–1–4448–3655–4

Published by
F. A. Thorpe (Publishing)
Anstey, Leicestershire

Set by Words & Graphics Ltd.
Anstey, Leicestershire
Printed and bound in Great Britain by
T. J. International Ltd., Padstow, Cornwall

This book is printed on acid-free paper

1

That fateful Monday morning dawned cold and blustery, and by the time Meg Warren arrived at St Nicholas's School for the Poor, it was sleeting heavily. By necessity, her usual short, unhurried walk from the horse-drawn tram to her destination had been more of a cautious dash today, but still her full plaid skirt and matching jacket were as wet through when she arrived as her straw 'cartwheel' hat and folding parasol.

Grimacing at the foul weather, she hurried up the stone steps to the school's double doors, and was just reaching for one of the polished brass handles to let herself inside when the right-hand door opened without warning and a tall, thin man in a long single-breasted morning coat and silk top hat stepped out into the storm.

Startled by his unexpected appearance,

Meg tilted her parasol back a little. Although she had never seen him before, she was just about to offer a polite smile when he brushed past her with hardly a glance, descended the steps and hurried off into the murk, the iron ferrule of his Malacca walking stick clacking impatiently against the pavement with every snowy step he took.

Taken aback by his lack of manners in an age when manners were still considered so very important, Meg paused a moment to watch him go. Despite the treacherous slush, his stride was quick and confident, and the neatly trimmed hair visible beneath his topper was as white as bone. He was clearly a man of some means, she decided, for his clothes were well tailored and of the highest quality, and for that reason alone, he appeared as out of place here in London's dismal East End as did she. As she finally let herself into the building, she wondered who he was and what business had brought him to the school. If only she had known . . .

The narrow corridor in which she found herself was dark and cheerless, but at least it was dry, and it was with a sense of relief that she hurried along to the glorified cupboard that masqueraded as the staff room, where she placed the now-closed parasol in a Butler's sink in one corner. Next she carefully peeled off her wide-brimmed now-soaking hat, and then hung her jacket on a hook on the back of the door.

It had long been Meg's custom to arrive early for work. She had learned very quickly that whilst teaching under-privileged children of all ages could be rewarding, it was rarely if ever easy. Some children found it impossible to apply themselves to their studies, while others were simply unwilling, considering 'book learning' to be a waste of time that might otherwise be spent more profitably in work. As a result, one or two of the older boys could be disruptive when they chose, though the majority understood that education was the means by which they might one day escape from their present wretched circumstances.

Thus, for Meg, preparation was everything. The children were always easily distracted, so it was crucial to make lessons as interesting and varied as possible. But just now, planning her program for the day would have to make way for simply drying herself off.

For want of something more suitable, Meg picked up a folded tea towel and went over to the small mirror hanging on the sickly green wall, where she set about drying her long auburn hair. At twenty years of age, she was a little above average height and of lithe build, with a pale, heart-shaped face dominated by expressive hazel-gray eyes. Usually, she wore her hair in the fashionable 'low pompadour' style of the day, which suited her well and was easy to maintain; but just now it was somewhat bedraggled, and dripping water from the tips.

She dried it as best she could, then used a brush and some pins from her embroidered handbag purse to make herself look as presentable as possible. As she worked, thunder made the tall, sleet-pebbled window buzz in its frame. Watching the icy rain fall, she suspected that a number of her ragamuffins — especially those over the age of ten, for whom schooling was not yet compulsory — would fail to show up for lessons today, blaming the weather.

At last she finished with her hair and went to a clanking cast-iron steam radiator to do what she could to dry off her skirt. She pinched at, and then lifted, the folds so that she could hold the material as close to the radiator as she dared, and the thick material was just beginning to steam when she heard the door open behind her. She glanced over one shoulder, then turned hurriedly, letting the skirt drop back to her ankles as she found herself looking into the face of the school's stern principal, Mrs. Amelia Hewitt.

'Good morning, ma'am,' she said, folding her hands in front of her.

From the very first, Mrs. Hewitt had insisted upon being addressed as 'ma'am'. She was a short, rotund woman of about fifty, with sagging jowls, a slightly yellow cast to her skin and constantly weary blue eyes. As always, the thick iron-gray hair she wore in a series of fussy Marcel waves radiating away from her arrow-straight center parting looked flawless.

'Good morning, Miss Warren,' she replied. There had never been any familiarity where Mrs. Hewitt was concerned. She liked everyone to know their place, and that just because two people happened to be colleagues, it should not necessarily follow that they must also be friends. 'I thought I might find you here this early. Please be so kind as to come to my office immediately.'

Meg nodded demurely. 'Of course, ma'am.'

But Mrs. Hewitt was already turning

away and closing the staff room door softly behind her. That was something else about the headmistress — when she gave an order, she expected it to be obeyed, and did not anticipate ever having to repeat it.

Just then another peal of thunder rumbled directly overhead, and it sounded so close that Meg actually flinched, fearing that the roof might come down on top of them. After all, the ancient building was hardly sound as it was, having been rented cheaply by a consortium of businessmen who had decided some years before to plow a small portion of their wealth into the creation of a school for the underprivileged. But against all odds, the walls continued to stand around her, and with her skirt still steaming, Meg left the room and went down the corridor toward Mrs. Hewitt's office. Here she knocked smartly and waited until the headmistress called, 'Enter.'

The headmistress's office, with its light cream walls, filled bookshelves, cheery fireplace and large framed portrait of the King hanging in pride of place on the wall behind her, was altogether more inviting than the staff room. Mrs. Hewitt herself sat behind a large mahogany desk that faced the door, and was just pouring tea from a delicate china pot into an equally delicate china cup, when Meg closed the door softly behind her and said, 'You wanted to see me, ma'am?'

Mrs. Hewitt nodded. 'Please, dear, come and sit down.'

Meg was momentarily taken aback. She thought, *Dear? Did she just call me . . . dear?* The headmistress was not given to using such terms of endearment, and for her to use one now made Meg feel strangely uneasy.

As she sat, Mrs. Hewitt said, 'How long have you been with us now, Miss Warren? Eight months, isn't it?'

'Yes, ma'am.'

'How time does fly,' Mrs. Hewitt observed.

'Yes, ma'am,' Meg repeated.

'And yet,' said Mrs. Hewitt regretfully, 'like all good things, it must eventually come to an end.'

Meg frowned. 'I'm sorry, ma'am . . . I don't understand.'

The headmistress looked uncomfortable now, and stirred nervously at her cup. 'As you know,' she said slowly, while thunder continued to rumble outside, 'we have limited means with which to conduct our good work. The board of governors give as much as they can to ensure that we may educate the poor to the best of our ability, but sadly, their pockets are not bottomless. They have other, perhaps more important, responsibilities, and to meet these, it is sometimes necessary that they rob Peter so that they may pay Paul.'

Meg's frown deepened. 'I'm sorry,' she said again. 'What are you trying to say, exactly?'

By Mrs. Hewitt's standards, such an interruption was an unforgivable breach of etiquette. She had never been interrupted in her life; she simply would not tolerate it. But to Meg's surprise, the headmistress showed no anger — she was too . . . what was it? Embarrassed? Guilty?

Whatever it was, she overlooked the intrusion and said bluntly: 'I am going to have to let you go, Miss Warren.'

The news was so unexpected that Meg could hardly believe her ears. She said, 'I . . . ' but then her voice trailed off as words deserted her.

'With immediate effect,' the headmistress added.

Meg shook her head, finding it difficult to process what she had just been told. 'Is this any reflection on my work?' she asked at last.

'None at all, dear,' said Mrs. Hewitt, and there was that word *dear* again. 'Your work has always been exemplary, as has your commitment to the children, your general deportment and your timekeeping. It is a . . . a simple case of economics. At the present time, we can no longer afford to employ you.'

Meg was now thoroughly bewildered.

'But . . . who will teach the children?' she asked, as if in a daze.

'I shall,' said Mrs. Hewitt.

In the silence that followed, all that could be heard was the persistent tap-tap-tap of sleet against the window.

'Should I . . . should I consider the situation as temporary?' Meg asked. 'I mean . . . will I be required again when the school is once more in funds?'

Mrs. Hewitt gave her a curious look, and Meg thought she saw a movement in the other woman's weary eyes that looked very close to the beginnings of a tear. But she couldn't have . . . *could* she? In all the time she had known Mrs. Hewitt, she had never seen any show of emotion, save perhaps anger and impatience. But perhaps she had underestimated the headmistress. Perhaps she *was* human, after all.

'I'm afraid not,' said Mrs. Hewitt softly. 'As I said, I am afraid I have to let you go with immediate effect. You will, of course, receive your salary for this week, even though you are no longer required. I wish it could have been more, but finances do not permit any show of *largesse* at present.' She looked down at her blotter and picked up one of two sealed envelopes, upon which she had written in her faultless script, *To Whom It May Concern*. 'I have prepared your references,' she said briskly. 'I think you will find them fair and generous.'

Numbly, Meg took the envelope. Her mind was awhirl. She had just lost the job she loved, a job that had become her whole life. She thought about the children she taught — little Dickie Palmer with his impish face and constant runny nose, and young Harriet Jackson, whom she had painstakingly taught to read and write, and who now read for pleasure just about everything Meg put in front of her. There was Miriam Rowe, who had lacked confidence until Meg gave her the encouragement that should by rights have come from her disinterested parents, and tow-headed Tommy Lawrence, who has been so self-conscious about his stammer until Meg had taught him to slow his rate of speech, and concentrate more on his breathing.

These and others — Jacob Woodmore, Raymond Lovejoy, Bridget Hopewell, Adela Bray — what would become of them now? She doubted that Mrs. Hewitt would have the patience to deal with them as compassionately as she had.

Suddenly she remembered the man who had brushed past her so rudely just a few minutes earlier; the tall, thin man with the bone-white hair and the Malacca walking stick. Had he been from the board of governors, then, come to instruct Mrs. Hewitt that she should dismiss her only member of staff in order to save money?

'Miss Warren?'

Meg blinked and sat a little straighter. 'I'm sorry, ma'am?'

'I said you do not have any family here in London, I believe?'

'No, ma'am. I don't have family anywhere. The children were . . . ' But she said no more.

'Then I may have a proposal for you,' said the headmistress hesitantly. 'It has . . . come to my knowledge that a family — a *good* family, I may add — is in need of a governess for their children, who are both seven years of age. The position is located out in the country, but since you have no obligations here . . . ' She paused. 'You don't, do you?'

'No, ma'am.'

'No . . . gentleman callers?'

'No, ma'am.'

'No one at all?'

'No, ma'am.'

'Then there is nothing to keep you here in London?' said Mrs. Hewitt.

It was a sad, indisputable truth. 'No, ma'am,' Meg said again, in a small voice.

Mrs. Hewitt seemed to realize what she had said, and added hastily, 'What I mean, dear, is . . . you would be free to take up the position I mentioned without . . . well, it's not as if you would be leaving anything behind you here.'

'No, ma'am,' Meg said softly. And it was true. Aside from her job, aside from the children who had come to mean as much if not more to her as any real family, she had no one who would miss her.

'The family I speak of,' said the headmistress, 'is one of good reputation, and the salary they have suggested to me is generous in the extreme. In addition, you would receive board and lodging. For the teaching of the two children — they are twin girls, apparently, named Achlys and Ahriman — you would be most handsomely rewarded — '

'I'm not concerned about the money,' Meg said, only vaguely aware that she had interrupted the headmistress yet again.

'No, no, of course not,' Mrs. Hewitt assured her quickly, and there could be no mistaking it now — the headmistress, usually so completely in control of herself, whatever the situation, was actually flustered. 'I know just how sincere you are, how seriously you take your responsibilities. I know that teaching is a true vocation for you. I just . . . ' She tailed off and stirred her tea some more. 'I . . . I regret that I have to let you go, and feel . . . obliged to make sure you have another position to go to. A good one. One that will reward you in a way that we here at St Nicholas's never really could.'

Meg nodded distantly. She had not been prepared to hear the unpleasant truths of her life, but they *were* true, nonetheless. Since the death of her mother and then her Aunt Rachel, she had no one — no family, no real friends. The school and its pupils had come to be her whole life; and it was a life she had found fulfilling, until this moment. She had wanted for nothing else, just these poor waifs and strays who deserved love, attention and encouragement that was not always to be found in their home lives.

And for the most part they had responded to that. She liked to think they held her in high regard. But more than that, that they *trusted* her. When all else seemed to be against them, she was always there for them, and perhaps naively believed she always would be.

Without her job at St Nicholas's, what else was left for her in the city? She could probably find similar employment elsewhere — as Mrs. Hewitt had told her, her references were good, to say the least. But perhaps it was high time for a change of scene. In her heart of hearts, she didn't really believe that, but she was determined to look upon the change in her circumstances positively, if she could.

'Very well,' she said. 'Thank you for thinking of me, ma'am. I should be happy to apply for the position you mentioned.'

'There is no need for that,' said the headmistress. 'The job is already yours.'

Meg's fine brows met above her small nose. 'You mean . . . there is no need for an interview?'

'No,' said Mrs. Hewitt. 'The family is happy to employ you upon . . . upon my recommendation.'

'Why, th-thank you,' said Meg, realizing that this was a compliment indeed.

'Then you will accept the position?' the headmistress asked eagerly.

The reply to that could only be another sad truth. 'I have nothing better to consider.'

Mrs. Hewitt's eyelids fluttered with relief. 'Thank you, dear. You will be satisfied with the arrangements, I am sure.'

'Where exactly will I be required to go?'

'Devon,' said Mrs. Hewitt. 'A village called Pendarren, to be precise. It is located on the eastern edge of Dartmoor, I believe.'

'It is,' Meg whispered, hardly able to believe her ears. 'It's the village in which I was born.'

Mrs. Hewitt raised her eyebrows. 'How fortunate for you, then! You already know your destination intimately.'

Meg hardly heard her. 'The family,' she said apprehensively. 'M-may I ask their name?'

'Averill,' the headmistress replied. 'Mr. Gerald Averill and his wife, Leona.

They occupy a property known as — '

'Stormview,' Meg interrupted; and for a moment, then, she actually thought she might faint.

Mrs. Hewitt saw the blood leach from her face and sat forward, genuine concern in her expression. 'Miss Warren,' she said sharply, 'are you all right?'

Meg nodded. It was as much as she could manage just then.

Stormview. She had all but forgotten the name, and what the place had come to represent to her. For an instant then it was on the tip of her tongue to say that she was sorry but she had changed her mind and could not possibly accept a job in such a house. But she had already given her word. She didn't feel she could let Mrs. Hewitt down by going back on it. Besides, it would be nice to revisit the quaint little village in which she had grown up. And it was high time she attempted to exorcise her dread of Stormview once and for all . . . or at least try to.

'Dear . . . ?' Mrs. Hewitt prompted.

19

Meg felt her senses settling again and took a deep, steadying breath. 'I'm fine. This . . . well, it has come as a shock, that's all.'

The headmistress nodded sympathetically. 'I am only sorry to have to let you go,' she replied, and really seemed to mean it. 'However, I must. Still, the chance to return to your roots, as it were . . . ' Overhead, thunder rumbled again, and the sleet began to tap even more insistently at the window. 'As the saying goes, every cloud has a silver lining, yes?'

'Yes,' Meg agreed, though she didn't especially believe it just then.

'Then you may get along,' said Mrs. Hewitt, standing, her tea untouched. 'I will inform the family that you will be with them at the earliest convenience, and then assume your duties from this morning onwards.'

Meg stood, somewhat shocked that she should leave so abruptly. 'Are you . . . sure you don't want me to work out the week?'

'There is no need for that, dear,' said the headmistress, and there was that *dear* again, the one that made her feel so uneasy every time she heard it. 'You may consider yourself free to take up your new position immediately. Indeed, I was so certain you would that I . . . took the liberty of arranging your rail passage to Devon.' So saying, she picked up the second envelope on her blotter and passed it over.

And that was how the life Meg had known and loved ended; and how a new, darker and more terrifying existence for her began.

2

It didn't take Meg long to settle her affairs in London. The only thing she really had to do was give notice — admittedly short notice — to her landlady. After that, all that remained was to pack her few belongings into a single suitcase and catch the early train from Paddington Station the following morning.

As the still-dark city fell behind her and the train slowly steamed west through the wakening suburbs, she stared through the carriage window without really seeing the vista beyond, and wondered if she had done the right thing in accepting the job. Under any other circumstances, she would have been excited at such a prospect. But it was its location that caused her misgivings. Indeed, even after all these years, she still hesitated even to *think* of the name Stormview. However, she had given her word, and once given she would never consider going back on it. That was her father's influence on her, of course.

Pendarren's village constable, Jacob Warren, had been a man of great principles, tall and broad-shouldered, with neat black hair and a well-tended handlebar moustache of the same hue. She could still see him well, even though it had been close to eleven years since he'd died. Those blue eyes that always seemed so serious and determined until the man broke into a smile or a grin that was simply too infectious to resist. The scent of his aftershave . . . nearly always witch hazel, but sometimes bay rum. The smell of his pipe tobacco — she still remembered the name of it . . . Golden Scepter. And when she thought about it, she could still hear his voice in her mind; that deep, measured tone that could be fiercely commanding when it needed to be, or kind when compassion was called for.

'All you have is your good name, pet,'

he had told her once. 'If you don't have that, you really don't have much of anything. So always say what you mean and mean what you say, and you won't go far wrong in life.' It was certainly the way he had always lived his own life. And it was doubtless why he had become such a diligent policeman.

Now, as the suburbs fell behind her and the new day continued to dawn cold and overcast, she recalled how he would check his appearance in the hallway mirror before going out on his regular patrols of the little town and its surroundings. He would brush imaginary lint from the dark blue lapels of his tunic and settle his cap at exactly the right angle on his head, then go out into the front garden, back ramrod-straight, and wheel his bicycle along the path to the gate, where he would always turn back to wave and wink and show her the grin that made him appear so much younger than he was.

She had always felt proud of him, because he was a policeman, and the rest of the village trusted him. Indeed, the locals frequently sought his guidance on all sorts of matters, and he never disappointed them. It was almost as if he'd lived before: No matter the problem, Jacob Warren would always offer the sagest advice to sort it out.

But then . . .

It still hurt to know that the only problems he had never been able to fix were his own — problems he kept strictly to himself and never confided to anyone. Perhaps if he had . . . But Meg knew from long experience that there was nothing to be gained from that line of thought. Still, if only he had opened up about whatever it was that had eventually led him to take his own life . . .

Until then, *her* life had been wonderful. She had enjoyed her schooling and had many friends. The village was a safe, picturesque environment in which to grow up — unlike the mean surroundings of her little and not-so-little charges at St Nicholas's, where it often seemed to her as if danger lurked in every corner. She had enjoyed a magical childhood . . . except for the afternoon she and her friends had decided to explore Stormview.

The suggestion had come from a sometimes abrasive boy named Russell Barber. At first, the others had stared at him as if he were mad, for by that time all manner of rumors had circulated about Vincent Averill and his strange, twisted house. Some said he raised the dead there at the stroke of midnight. Others claimed he was in league with the Devil, who visited him regularly. Meg's father had always told her that the plain and simple truth was that Averill preferred his own company.

'Why does he prefer that, Da?' she had asked at the time.

He'd shrugged. 'Do you like spinach?' he replied.

She wrinkled her nose. 'I hate it!'

'Well, me — I love it,' he said. 'And that's the way it is with people. We're all different. Some like company. They're never happier than when they have people around them, laughing and chatting and being the center of attention. Others, like old Vincent Averill . . . they like to keep to themselves. More often than not, there's no reason to it; it's just the way it is. And you should never judge someone just because he or she is different to you. Remember, it's all those differences that make the world such an interesting place.'

It was good advice. But somehow her unease whenever she saw or thought about Stormview never quite left her. Vincent Averill, a widower, was seldom seen in the village, any more than his son, Gerald. And when they did appear, they seldom stayed long and never socialized. They acted with the arrogance of masters over servants, and treated everyone they perceived to be of a lower class as mere cattle. Worse still, they didn't seem to care who knew it. But it went deeper than that. There were those rumors, and as a child of nine, Meg could be forgiven for believing even the most outlandish of them.

The house itself did little to dispel the aura of strangeness that always seemed to cling to Averill and his son. The story went that Averill, having made a fortune in business, had decided to retire to the countryside. He had bought land in a valley a mile or so outside Pendarren and then brought in an architect to design his new home. But the architect's plans were not what Averill wanted, so he decided to redesign the place himself. The end result was a vile, twisted thing, built in no particular style and with no sense of balance or aesthetics. It was said that just looking at Stormview's crooked lines could make one feel dizzy, or as if the world had somehow tilted underfoot. There was one saving grace, however. Whether or not it was something to do with the location — that isolated bowl of land surrounded by dense woods — the house was nearly always obscured by a curtain of mist.

At Russell Barber's suggestion, the children — there were six of them that day, three boys, three girls — stared at each other with wide eyes and open mouths. Explore Stormview! The very idea filled Meg with fear. And yet, as she looked at her companions, she could see that they were fascinated by the prospect. Another boy, David Sparks, said quickly, 'Yes!' But still there was some hesitancy in the rest of the group.

'What if old Averill catches us?' asked a girl named Susan Brown.

'He won't,' Russell replied confidently. 'We'll be so quiet he'll never even know we were there. Anyway, I'm not saying we actually go *into* the house, even if we could. Just as close as we dare, and have a look around.'

'That's trespassing,' Meg heard herself telling them. 'If we got caught, we could get sent to prison.'

Russell gave her a sneer. 'Don't be daft. We're too young for that.'

'Anyway,' said David Sparks, 'Russell's right. We won't get caught. We'll be too clever.'

'I'm game,' said Susan Brown, who

had always been a bit of a tomboy.

'And me,' said David.

'And me,' said a girl called Denise Ackland.

'That makes four,' said Russell. 'Come on, Meg. It'll be fun.'

Meg could hardly see how it could be that. Still she wavered until the third boy in their little group said gently, 'It's all right, Meg. I'll look after you.'

Meg looked over at the speaker. Adam Eden was a tall boy about a year older than her, with thick chestnut-brown hair brushed to the right and dark well-proportioned features. Funny and intelligent, he also had a gentle, sensitive nature she had always found appealing. And as she looked at him now, she saw perfect understanding in his bright, chocolate-brown eyes. He knew she was scared, and far from seeing that as a sign of weakness, or an excuse to tease her, he wanted only to offer comfort and support. Not for the first time, she thought shyly that it would be very easy to love him.

'All right,' she said. And with that, they set off.

The autumn afternoon had been bright but crisp, the sky a deep, vivid blue. Russell led the way and the other children followed, most of them enjoying an almost delicious sense of frightened anticipation at what they were about to do. Meg hung back, and Adam automatically fell into step beside her.

'Don't worry,' he said quietly. 'I won't let anything happen to you.'

She glanced up at him almost bashfully. 'Thank you.'

'You don't have to thank me. I'm just saying . . . I'll make sure no harm comes to you.'

By then the rutted cedar-lined lane had given way to Serenity Bridge, an arched wooden span that provided a crossing point above a tributary known locally as Mare's Tail Beck, for the wild but pleasant bottlebrush flowers that grew in abundance along its banks. Here, at this local landmark, it was easy for Meg to tell herself she was being silly, and worrying far too much over nothing. Stormview was just a house, no more. But as they went over the gentle hump of the bridge, she felt its ancient beams creaking and shifting ominously underfoot, and wished she could turn back. Adam wouldn't mind. He would probably turn back with her, if only to keep her company. But the others ... they would taunt her mercilessly and call her a coward.

Then the bridge was behind them and the valley awaited them up ahead. The air seemed somehow colder than it had been just seconds earlier, and the lane and the thick woods that hemmed it in on two sides began to blur imperceptibly with the almost ever-present mist that lingered there.

With a suddenness that was startling, that same mist abruptly surrounded them, and all at once every sound seemed strangely muted. The other children, who had been laughing and chattering and trying to scare each other on the walk from the village, now fell silent, almost as if they, too, were regretting the course they had set for themselves.

Trees — they were pines now, plus weirdly shaped monkey puzzles and pagoda trees with long hanging fronds — shouldered in on either side of them, their questing branches seen only dimly through the yellow fog as they clawed skyward. There was no birdsong, just oppressive silence and the soft shush-shush of their footsteps against the stunted grass.

'Russell . . . ' Denise Ackland called. She made the name sound more like a whine.

'Scared?' Russell jeered over one shoulder.

'No!' Denise replied vehemently. 'I just . . . well . . . what if we *do* get caught? Who's to say they *won't* put us in prison?'

'We won't get caught,' replied Russell, adding casually, 'Of course, you can always turn back if you want to.'

'I don't want to!' Denise cried, although it was clear from her tone that she did, very much so.

Meg said, 'If you want to go back, I'll go with you.'

Denise looked back at her. 'No,' she said. 'It . . . it's all right.'

The bulk of the woods now lay behind them. Up ahead, the fog thinned somewhat, and as they gathered on the little ridge that led down into the valley itself, they finally saw their destination waiting for them.

Stormview.

The house itself was an ugly central block of earth-colored bricks that stood three stories tall, with small paired windows and a balcony fashioned from black wrought-iron scrollwork that ran along the first floor. A central overhang thrust out from the roof and was supported by four vast columns that were, when you got close enough, actually a series of thin columns all clustered together in the Gothic style. A single square tower rose from the center of the roof, with three long, narrow windows in each face, save for the fourth, in which were set four.

At each of the four corners of the roof stood a round tower with a spired roof, each spire just that little bit skewed to one side. Above every door and window, a stone arch was raised like a startled eyebrow. And the low wall that ran around the lip of the roof was home to a positive menagerie in stone — a series of waterspouts disguised as gargoyles and dragons and other winged or reptilian-looking creatures that might or might not have existed in some prehistoric era.

The children stared at the place for a long time, in awe of its strangeness. Looking at it, it appeared to be empty and lifeless, its curtained windows dull and blind. But who could say for sure? Someone might be in there, watching them, even now.

'Come on,' said Russell, and somewhat reluctantly, the other children followed him as he descended the slope toward the house.

The sun seldom penetrated the valley to any great degree, so the grass was still slick with dew, and they had to take care on its slippery surface. Still there were no other sounds in the valley but their own. Meg tried to convince herself that the Averills were out somewhere, in which case all they had to worry about was the staff. If they ran at the first sign of discovery, they should be all right.

But thinking of the staff made her think of John Claydon, who acted as Vincent Averill's combination butler, valet and coachman. A big man with jowly features, he had a round drinker's nose, sour lips and gray eyes that sat in tired pouches of skin. He looked much older than his thirty years, and was bald but for some thinning reddish-brown hair that encircled his shining pate. On the few times she had seen him, he had always struck her as being a humorless man who showed as much contempt for those around him as did his master.

If John Claydon should see and catch

them, she felt they could expect no mercy at all.

At last they reached the valley floor. Around them, the mist swirled and pulsed, and seemed to have an evil, sulfurous smell to it, like charred wood. They gathered in the cover of some bushes about fifty yards from the house, and David Sparks said in a breathless whisper, 'Now what?'

That was a very good question. Everyone looked at Russell, who said, rather lamely, 'Well . . . we explore.' When they continued to look at him, he added, 'You know. Have a look around.'

'There's a sort of barn affair over there, on the far side of the house,' Susan Brown pointed out. 'We could see what's inside it.'

The barn stood about fifty yards away, and perhaps thirty yards from the house itself. It was a tall, wide, ramshackle affair, its lines as tilted and unequal as those of Stormview itself, patchwork in appearance for having been built from what looked like reclaimed wood, with no two planks obtained from the same source.

Russell nodded. 'Yes, that's where we'll start.' And his eyes lit up as he added, 'I bet that's where old Averill keeps all the dead bodies he summons to keep Satan happy!'

'Russell!' snapped Adam. 'That's not funny.'

'Oh, I've scared you too, have I?' asked Russell. Then he remembered that Adam's father had died several years earlier, when Adam himself had been little more than a babe in arms, and looked contrite.

'I'm just saying, that's all,' he said. 'You shouldn't talk about the dead like that. And you should certainly watch what you say about Satan.'

Unable to meet his eyes, Russell slipped from cover and began to run toward the barn, crouched over in an attempt to avoid detection. The others followed suit. They reached the side of the barn safely and stood there for a little while, getting their breath back.

Still Meg kept her attention focused on the house, which crouched like a malevolent watchdog at the end of a narrow, crooked track that led right to the front steps.

Russell gestured that they should be quiet so that he could listen at a gap in the plank walls.

'Can you hear anything?' Denise Ackland asked fearfully.

Russell shook his head, then put his eye to the gap. After another moment he said, 'I can see what looks like a carriage, but that's about all. And no, I can't hear anything. Still, the dead don't make much noise, do they?' Now he did look at Adam, daring him to say something.

'This was a silly idea to begin with,' David Sparks said suddenly. 'I'm going home.'

'I was only joking,' Russell said placatingly. 'Look, we're here now. At least let's have a look inside.'

Without waiting for their agreement, he tiptoed to the corner of the barn and, against their better judgment, the others followed behind him. Around the corner they crept, until they reached the big double doors, which were held shut by a crude wooden bar. Even as Russell reached for it, Denise Ackland hissed, 'Wait! I thought I heard something!'

'Course you didn't,' said Russell. 'You imagined it.'

'No, it was a growl.' She gestured anxiously toward the barn. 'It came from in there.'

'Well, *I* didn't hear it.'

'Neither did I,' offered David.

'But what if it's a dog? What if it bites one of us?'

Russell shook his head in exasperation. 'Oh, don't be so silly!' Again he reached for the bar, but this time they all heard it — a low, drawn-out growl coming from inside the barn.

'It *is* a dog,' breathed David.

'It might even be a wolf,' suggested Susan.

'Or a werewolf,' whispered Denise.

Again Russell started to tell her not to be so silly, when suddenly he froze. 'Listen!'

'What is — '

'Shhh!'

Although it was barely audible, they all heard it, then . . . the faint but unmistakable sound of someone — several people, actually — chanting.

'Who is it?' asked David.

'It's coming from the house,' Adam said grimly.

'What are they saying?'

'It's all nonsense words,' said Russell.

Meg shook her head. 'It sounds like Latin to me.'

Even as she finished speaking, they heard the ponderous, mournful tolling of a bell floating on the mist. They all looked at each other, wide-eyed, and Meg thought, *I knew we shouldn't have come here, I knew it!*

Adam said, 'That's definitely coming from the tower.' And he pointed toward the square but crooked tower that rose from the center of Stormview's roof.

'He's right,' said David, his voice hushed. 'I think we ought to get out of here.'

'Me too,' said Denise, suddenly close to tears.

Secretly Russell wanted to get out of there, too, but since this had been his idea to begin with, he felt he should show some leadership. 'There's no need for that,' he said as authoritatively as he could manage.

'But that chanting — '

'Probably just — ' Before he could offer an explanation, there came another ominous growl from the other side of the barn doors, and David stabbed a finger toward the house. 'Look! Some-one's coming!'

The others looked in the direction he had indicated and saw several figures coming from around the back of the large house. They were walking slowly, in single file, and to Meg they looked like monks, for they all wore long tar-black robes and cowls — at least that was her impression; the mist had a peculiar way of altering shapes and distance.

Inside the barn, the dog or wolf or whatever it was began to throw itself against the doors. That, coupled with the mournful tolling of the bell and the slow-moving hooded figures who might as well have been phantoms, was enough.

'*Run!*'

It was Russell's voice, now sounding high and panicky. Not waiting for the others, he sprinted for the bushes and the slope beyond. Adam grabbed Meg's hand, and as one, all of them ran after Russell. Meg thought she heard someone yell, though she was well aware that it might just have been her overwrought imagination playing a trick on her. Then they were all laboring up the slope and back to the questionable safety of the woods.

The climb took far longer than the descent. The boys quickly overtook the girls. But gradually the ridge and the woods beyond came closer, closer . . .

Then, without warning, Meg lost her footing on the dew-wet grass and cried out as pain seared through her left ankle. She tumbled to her knees and immediately tried to get back up, but it was impossible — the pain from her twisted ankle was too severe.

For a moment then blind terror held her in its thrall. The dirge-like tolling of the bell seemed to gather momentum, the chanting of the hooded figures sounded louder, and the growling and snapping of whatever was locked in the barn was somehow sharper, as if the creature had suddenly gained its freedom or been set loose.

Then a figure appeared out of the mist and reached for her. She cried out again as a hand closed on her arm. But then Adam was saying, 'It's all right, Meg. I've got you.'

At the sound of his voice her panic receded, albeit just a little. Somehow her vision cleared and she found herself looking up at him. His face looked so serious, so earnest. In the next moment he was helping her to her feet, and she was leaning on him and they were trying to climb the remainder of the slope together. Of Russell and the others there was now no sign.

Behind them, the bell continued to strike the same monotonous note, and whatever creature the Averills had locked in the barn continued to growl and snap. Meg chanced a look over one shoulder and saw the doors alternately shaking and bulging outwards as something threw itself at them from the inside. Then Adam was urging her on up the slope, and she was limping worse than ever.

A second later, Adam lost his own footing and went to his knees. Meg went down beside him. She looked at him, but saw no fear in him — what she saw was his determination, fiercer now than ever, to protect her. 'You go on,' he said, and standing again, he turned back to face Stormview, now reduced to the size of a doll's house by distance. 'I'll make sure they don't come after you.'

She stared at him. He was so solemn, so intense, that she realized he would indeed face whatever was behind them, so long as it meant he could save her from whatever it might be.

'I'm not going without you,' she said; and something happened then, something strange and completely unforeseen. As they looked at each other, a bond formed between them that was felt by both. It was so strong that tears sprang to Meg's eyes as she realized how important it was, how important *he* was, and how important she evidently was to him.

For a moment he was caught in indecision. But then he looked back down toward Stormview and said, 'Listen.'

'What is it?' she asked, her voice low.

'That bell,' he whispered back. 'It's stopped ringing.'

She realized it was true. Furthermore, the dog had also fallen quiet, and the chanting had ended. They looked long and hard, but of the mysterious figures in their robes and cowls there was no sign.

She thought it was impossible that they could have imagined all of it. Some, yes, but not everything. And yet it seemed that they now had the valley all to themselves, save of course for the malevolent presence of Stormview itself.

Adam flopped down beside her. Relieved, she allowed herself to sag against him; and as if it were the most natural thing in the world, he put an arm around her and gave her shoulders a squeeze. 'I think we're all right now,' he murmured.

They both grew aware of their closeness then, and almost jumped apart. Blushing, Adam quickly got back to his feet and reached down to her. 'Come on,' he said.

She took his hand and carefully climbed to her feet.

'Lean on me,' he told her, and that was how they completed the remainder of the climb.

Yes, she thought. He would be very easy to love. But until this moment she had never dreamed just *how* easy.

3

Somehow, Meg must have fallen asleep during the long journey to Devon, for the next thing she knew, the train was slowing and it was early afternoon, though still cool and overcast. At once she sat a little straighter, embarrassed that she had dozed off, and grateful that she had had the carriage to herself, for propriety's sake.

The village of Pendarren was slowly slipping past on the other side of the glass; Pendarren, with its cobbled roads and rows of whitewashed houses with neat blue trim, thatched roofs or mossy slate tiles. And it had hardly changed a bit. Although the streets appeared deserted, the shops she remembered so well from her childhood were all still there, the familiar signs hanging above their narrow doors swaying in the stiff wind — and there also was the centerpiece of the village, the beam-encrusted tavern, The Old George, looking just as fresh as a new penny!

Seeing everything so untouched by time gave her a strange choked feeling. She was immediately glad to be back, despite the sad memories the village held for her, and for the first time she began to feel that her time at Stormview might not be as bad as she had first feared.

With a wrenching of brakes, the train finally shuddered to a halt and she collected her luggage, such as it was, and climbed down to the platform. In summer, the station had been a riot of color, for the stationmaster, old Mr. Sawyer, always took such pride in his little domain and placed flowering tubs and hanging baskets everywhere. Now, of course, it was winter, Mr. Sawyer was long retired or perhaps even deceased, and the platform was mostly gray, save for little patches of frosty white snow that had gathered in sheltered corners and limned the black railings.

Behind her, the train gave a strident whistle that made her flinch a little. And as she turned to watch it leave, she shivered, for its departure made her feel almost as if she were being abandoned. The carriages rumbled across the level crossing down at the far end of the platform and then vanished into a low, dreary mist.

The happiness she had felt at seeing Pendarren again began to fade as a sense of isolation claimed her. Before it could overwhelm her completely, she left the station and stepped out onto the main street. As she did so, she caught a movement from the corner of her eye, and turning in that direction was just in time to see a man in a blue uniform vanishing around a corner perhaps fifty yards away. At once she pulled up short. For just a moment it might have been her father, patrolling the village exactly as he used to.

Of course, that was just an illusion, a case of her seeing what she would have loved to have seen just then. In any case, the man — the *policeman* — was no longer to be seen. Still, the sight of that beloved uniform gave her a sense of comfort when she felt she needed it most.

Hoping to spot a familiar face, she looked to left and right, but the street was still empty, for the keen wind blowing from the north made it a miserable day to be out. She had been assured by Mrs. Hewitt that someone would be at the station to meet her, but she could see no sign of a coach anywhere.

'Miss Warren?'

The voice came from directly behind her, and she turned quickly, her mouth a startled O. She found herself looking up into the face of John Claydon.

Vincent Averill's combination butler, valet and coachman had changed hardly at all. He was still the big jowly man she remembered from childhood, his eyes still flat and lackluster, his nose still the ruddy pitted strawberry that signified the heavy drinker. Now in his forties, he looked much older, and thoroughly ravaged by the life he had led. He looked down at her with no expression at all, and she herself could only look back up at him and remember how scared she had always been of him.

'Mr. Claydon,' she managed at last.

He looked surprised. 'You *remember* me?'

'Y-yes.' She felt a little lightheaded, being so close to him after all this time, and it reflected in her voice, which now sounded very small.

He took her suitcase and used it to gesture that she should follow him across the street. She saw then that he had parked the coach in a little alleyway, out of sight. But how he had managed to approach her without being seen, she had no idea.

'I hope you had a comfortable journey,' he said politely.

And there, she told herself suddenly, was the one change in him. There was nothing of his old swagger now, nothing of the contempt in which he had always held others. His manner was quiet, respectful, and though he retained his size and bulk, he no longer appeared especially threatening. Indeed, if anything, he reminded her of a man whose spirit had been thoroughly broken.

'I did, thank you,' she replied; and because she felt obliged to make conversation, she added, 'You stayed on after Mr. Averill died, then?'

He nodded. 'Master Gerald made it plain that I should.'

The black Clarence coach he had driven stood at the edge of the pavement, with two equally dusky horses in the traces. He made short work of stowing her case beneath the driver's seat and then opened the door so that she could enter the coach. It was only when the door closed behind her that she realized just how nice it was to get out of the biting wind. He climbed up onto the seat. She heard him call something to the team, and then the coach jerked into motion. Pendarren fell behind them.

Fingers knitting nervously, she looked out onto the surrounding countryside. Time really had stood still in her absence — everything was still so familiar and unchanged. She wondered if the same would apply to Gerald Averill and Stormview.

At length they came to Mare's Tail Beck, and she heard the horses' hooves clatter against the planks of Serenity Bridge. Although she couldn't be sure, the span seemed no safer now than it had been when she and her friends had crossed it on their way to explore Stormview all those years earlier. But now the bridge held other, far more painful memories for her. For it was here that her father had taken his own life. He had thrown himself off the bridge and into the beck, and the icy water had quickly numbed him and taken him deep into its depths.

A soft sob escaped her at the memory. It sounded loud in the confines of the coach. She still missed her father dreadfully, and was no closer to understanding why he had taken his own life now than she had been all those years ago. She had tried so hard to recall any times when he might have seemed in low spirits or preoccupied, but to her he had always been so bright and positive and in command. She knew now, of course, just how mistaken she had been, for something had clearly weighed heavily upon him. If she had only known what that something was, she might have better understood what had driven him to suicide.

She sat forward and stared out at the bridge. This was where he had spent his final moments, she reminded herself. What had gone through his mind as he'd looked down into the water? Had he seen his own reflection staring back up at him, and in that image all the problems for which he had no answers?

And yet still she found it hard to believe that he could have killed himself. Jacob Warren simply had not been built that way; she would stake her life upon it. He would have faced his problems head on, and never done anything to hurt the wife and daughter he loved so much.

Then the bridge was behind them and she sat back again, wishing as she always did that she could have understood a little more about her father, and what had happened to him that day, and why. After he died, she hadn't liked to broach the subject with her mother, who had taken his death even harder than she. In any case, how was a nine-year-old girl supposed to understand the complexities of being a grown-up? So she had kept her silence and tried to work it all out for herself, and watched her mother grow old before her eyes, with grief, and loss, and confusion.

Within a day of his death, the rumors had started. Jacob Warren had a drink problem, they said, and though he'd kept it well hidden, it had grown worse over the years until it became almost uncontrollable. It was absolute nonsense, of course; nothing more than spiteful gossip. Jacob Warren might have had a sherry at Christmas, but he had never been a drinker. He'd never really liked the taste of alcohol, and aside from that one bottle of sherry in the kitchen cupboard, the level of which never seemed to go down save for that one drink every Christmas Day, there was no other drink in the house.

No — whatever had led her father to take his own life, it had not been drink. But the rumor took hold, and it seemed to her that people were happier to believe the lie than to acknowledge the truth — that no one really knew what had driven him to do it.

And yet sympathy, of a sort, had come from an unexpected quarter. A few days after her father had committed suicide, Meg had been in her room when there had come a brisk rapping at the front door. Knowing that her mother was in no fit state to receive visitors, she had raced to answer it, only to rear back almost immediately as she identified their caller.

It was Vincent Averill. He was a tall, skeletal man in a spotless black suit. He was about sixty-five then, but like John Claydon, looked much older. His yellowish skin was mottled and hung loose against his skull. His eyes were heavy-lidded, and so dark they might have been almost all pupil. He had a long nose, a lean mouth, a sharp chin — a man with no gentle lines about him at all.

He had looked down at her for a moment, and she was so scared of him that she almost forgot to breathe. She could think of only one reason why he had come to call — to complain about the time that she and her friends had tried to explore Stormview. She had always believed they had escaped detection that day, but now Averill's presence here seemed to suggest otherwise.

His eyes held no vestige of warmth as he regarded her. Unable to meet his gaze, she had looked past him, to the coach that stood in the lane beyond the little gate, and John Claydon, standing by the nearside front wheel, staring back at her from an impassive face.

Then Averill had taken off his hat to reveal some thin flyaway hair the color of mud, and he said in that slow, deliberate way of his, 'I should like to see your mother.'

Meg had looked up at him, eyes wide.

With a hint of impatience, he said again, 'Your mother?'

Then Mrs. Warren was behind her, having heard the knock. She put her hands on Meg's shoulders, squeezed encouragingly, and said, almost as if she couldn't believe the evidence of her own eyes, 'Mr. Averill?'

He inclined his head imperiously. 'I wonder if I might impose upon you for a few moments, Mrs. Warren,' he said. His voice was soft, almost hypnotic, and seemed to Meg to hold the same quality as crumbling parchment. 'I should like to offer my condolences on your recent loss.'

Meg looked up at her mother. Mrs. Warren's expression was impossible to read. She appeared as taken aback by the request as she had been by his unexpected appearance, and Meg couldn't blame her. Vincent Averill was, as her father had told her, 'different'. He only ever came to the village when he had to, and had never shown any love for its inhabitants.

'Run along, Meg,' said Mrs. Warren after a moment. And then, stepping to one side, 'Please, Mr. Averill. May I . . . can I get you a cup of tea?'

Meg didn't hear his response. Just glad for the opportunity to escape his presence, she had hurried back to her bedroom.

As for what transpired during their meeting, she had no idea. She remembered that it was short — she doubted if Averill stayed longer than five minutes. And when he was gone, Mrs. Warren seemed more distraught than before. Indeed, it was shortly after that that she announced her intention to move them both to London, where they would live with her sister, Meg's widowed Aunt Rachel.

'Steady, there!'

John Claydon's voice, calling out to the two-horse team, brought her back from her thoughts, and she sat forward nervously, realizing all at once that the journey was almost over, and the coach was trending down into the fog-filled valley that cradled Stormview like some malign tumor. All at once her heart was in her mouth, for this was the moment she had dreaded more than any other — seeing Stormview again.

And it did not disappoint.

The years had not been kind to the house. The central tower and the four round towers at each corner were as skewed as they had ever been, and evoked a giddying sense of vertigo for the onlooker. Ivy had grown up across the earth-colored brick walls and hung limply from the wrought-iron scroll-work that ran along the first floor. The lace-hung windows looked dull, and barely reflected what little light there was on this blustery afternoon. And as for the gargoyles and dragons and other reptilian creatures that doubled as waterspouts around the lip of the roof, they were now stained with some sort of noxious green algae.

She turned her head and saw the decrepit barn, looking ghostly through the haze. The roof had sagged in on itself and appeared to be in an even worse state of repair now than it had all those years ago. For one fleeting instant, she remembered the creature that had thrown itself at its barred doors, so determined to get out, and the mournful tolling of the bell in the central tower, and the line of hooded figures appearing from the back of the house, half-obscured by the mist. After so many years, it should have been easy to dismiss the memories as the overwrought imaginings of a group of children who had only seen what they had half-feared, half-expected to see. And yet it *had* happened. She *knew* it had.

The coach came to a halt, and John Claydon climbed down and opened the door for her. She forced a smile for him, but he didn't return it. He seemed somehow nervous, agitated. But she thought she knew why that must be. Unlike her father, Claydon *was* a drinker. Perhaps it was a drink he craved now.

She looked around, noticing for the first time a bright crimson automobile that was parked to one side of the house. She had heard of such vehicles but never actually seen one before. It had two neatly upholstered seats facing each other, with some sort of tiller affair, which she assumed must be used for steering, positioned between them.

'It's called a De Dion Bouton,' offered Claydon, seeing the object of her interest and stumbling a little over the vehicle's French name. 'It's his most cherished possession.'

Then he collected her case from beneath his seat, and together they went up the steps to the column-flanked entranceway. Before they reached the door, however, it swung open and a middle-aged housekeeper in starched black and white inclined her head.

'Miss Warren,' she said, her tone carefully neutral. 'The master and mistress are expecting you.'

There was a momentary hesitation then, as Meg prepared herself to step across the threshold and enter this house of which she had always been so terrified. The housekeeper gave her an odd look, which she pretended not to see. Then, steeling herself, she stepped inside and found herself in a great old-fashioned hall with dark wainscoting, and being watched from the walls by stags' heads with sightless eyes.

A grand staircase with heavy oak balustrades led the way upstairs, illuminated by the light that filtered through an enormous stained-glass window that would have easily been large enough for an average-sized church. She followed the housekeeper across the herringbone-patterned floor, discovering as she did so that Stormview was a conductor of echoes, which floated up to the vaulted ceiling, there to multiply.

Then she was shown through a set of double doors and into a large room dominated by a vast fireplace, where in olden days she felt sure it would have been possible to roast an entire bullock. The room was expensively furnished with a scattering of upholstered French armchairs and sofas, a heavily inlaid writing desk, several mahogany display cabinets filled with books, and a *demi lune* card table upon which sat a gramophone. A three-panel screen stood in one corner, next to a chaise longue upon which sat a profusion of Victorian dolls. Painted landscapes hung from a dado rail, but they were all of dark, dismal forests and stagnant pools. The only real color of any note came from the Oriental rugs that had been thrown across a floor of highly polished wooden blocks.

A man and a woman stood beside the huge fireplace, watching her. She had no trouble recognizing Gerald Averill.

His likeness to his father was uncanny. He stood tall and angular in a black suit and brocade cravat, a man of sharp lines and those same piercing eyes that were so dark they might just as well have been all pupil. He was in his early thirties, his brown hair still thick and swept back from a high forehead, his features distinguished but too unrelentingly cheerless to ever be handsome.

'Miss Warren,' he said, and stepped forward to offer one soft, long-fingered hand that was cool to the touch. 'How very nice to meet you at last. May I present my wife, Leona?'

Leona was tall and slim, with a painfully thin face framed by a rich spill of glossy midnight-black hair that cascaded to her shoulders. Dressed in a gauzy gray and white dress trimmed with grosgrain ribbon, Meg judged her to be of an age with her husband, but her face was ghostly pale, her dark eyes somehow slightly vacant.

'I'm sure you will be very happy with us,' she said. 'I trust your journey was a pleasant one? Well, as pleasant as is possible in such inclement weather?'

'Yes, indeed.'

'And that returning to Pendarren has brought with it many happy memories?'

There was the faintest hesitation before she said, 'Yes.'

An uncomfortable silence settled between them after that. To break it, Meg said, 'I'm looking forward to meeting your children.'

At last some animation showed in Leona's eyes. 'The children,' she repeated. 'Oh, yes. They — '

'They are not here at present,' Gerald said, interrupting her. His voice was the voice of his father's — soft, slow, almost hypnotic, and with something about it that seemed incredibly old. 'They are staying with relatives, but we expect them back within a few days.'

'Achlys and Ahriman,' said Meg, more to make conversation than anything else. 'They're very unusual names.'

'They're very unusual *children*,'

Leona explained proudly.

'Well, as I say, I look forward to meeting them.'

'And in the meantime,' said Gerald, 'you may use your time to settle in and prepare your curriculum.'

'I will,' she agreed. 'As you are doubtless aware, it is not customary to begin a child's formal education until the age of ten, so engaging the minds of two seven-year-olds will be quite a challenge.'

'I am sure you will find them most well-behaved,' said Leona.

'Now,' said Gerald, 'there are one or two . . . formalities I must deal with, and for which I beg your indulgence.'

'I have references — '

'You are quite suitable in that respect.'

'Then . . . ?' She frowned, not quite understanding what he meant.

He looked at her for a long moment before he said, 'You are twenty years of age, I believe?'

'Yes. In fact, I will be twenty-one on Thursday.'

'Excellent,' he said, and smiled briefly. 'We shall do our best to ensure that your birthday is a memorable one.'

'Oh, there's no need for that — '

'Nonsense! It is the day you come of age, Miss Warren. We will find a way to mark the occasion.' Again he fell quiet. All that could be heard was the ponderous ticking of a yellow-faced grandfather clock in one alcove. 'There is, however, one further formality to which I must attend,' he said at length. 'And once again, I can only beg your indulgence.'

'Of course,' she said uncertainly.

'We are a somewhat ... spiritual family, Miss Warren. And as such, we insist upon a certain degree of ... convention. Of ... *chastity*, if you will.'

'I'm not sure I understand.'

He said bluntly, 'Are you a virgin, Miss Warren?'

At first she wasn't sure that she'd heard him correctly. When he realized that she had, she was stunned by the question, and it showed in her expression.

'I apologize for the indelicacy of my enquiry,' he continued. 'However, you must understand that we need to assure ourselves as to the . . . moral suitability of the person to whom we entrust the education of our children.'

Cheeks flushing, it was on the tip of Meg's tongue to tell Gerald that she found his question rude in the extreme and the implication that she might be anything other than chaste positively insulting. But then reason prevailed. It was in all likelihood exactly as he had said: that the family held to certain religious beliefs and standards, and if that was indeed the case then she must respect them, no matter how intrusive she might find them.

'You need not concern yourself on the matter,' she said stiffly.

He seemed relieved. 'Thank you,' he said, and moved to the bell-pull. 'Now, I will have Angela see you to your quarters, and allow you to rest after your journey. We serve afternoon tea at five. I trust you will join us?'

She nodded, wanting only to leave the room now. 'Of course,' she replied. 'You may instruct me as to the direction you would like the twins' education to take.'

4

The housekeeper, Angela, showed her up the wide staircase and along a first-floor hallway that seemed to go on forever. From the outside, the house had appeared large: from inside, it seemed positively enormous. The walls were paneled with oak, stained dark, and they reminded her of the walls of a maze as she continued to follow the housekeeper around a corner to the right. About halfway along this hallway, the housekeeper finally stopped and opened a door, then stepped aside so that she might enter first.

'If there is anything you need,' the housekeeper informed her, indicating a bell pull beside the door, 'you have only to ring.'

'Thank you.'

The housekeeper left without another word, closing the door softly behind her.

Meg allowed herself to sag a little. Entering this house and meeting Gerald and his wife had taken more out of her than she had dreamed. She took off her hat and unbuttoned her jacket, and went across the room to flop down on the edge of the bed, exhausted more emotionally than physically.

The room itself was comfortable enough, and there was a smell to the air that struck her as being familiar and reassuring, though she could not immediately identify it. In addition to the bed, there was a dressing table, a chest of drawers, a writing bureau and a heavy wardrobe before which someone — probably John Claydon — had left her suitcase. A low fire burned in a fireplace at the end of the room.

But it did no good. She stood up, took her coat off and hung it in the wardrobe. She didn't want to feel quite as hopeless as she did just then, but there was no help for it — when she thought about the children at St Nicholas's, of her cozy little lodgings in

London, of the pleasant way her life had gone along until the previous morning when her job had been taken away from her . . .

And yet there was nothing to be gained by feeling sorry for herself. She went to the fire and used the poker from the companion set to stir the blaze up a little. That made things somewhat cheerier for her, but when she went to the window and looked outside, all she could see was the drifting, faintly yellow mist, and she wondered how anyone could stand to live here for long and not begin to feel even a little claustrophobic.

She was thinking that when a voice just behind her whispered, 'Never . . . '

Taken by surprise, she heeled around quickly, wondering why the housekeeper hadn't knocked before entering — but then froze as she realized she was still all alone.

She stood still for a long moment. She *had* heard a voice . . . hadn't she? She would almost swear to it. Almost.

But she had been distracted, her mind elsewhere, her nerves still tense. That being the case, she couldn't say for certain.

In an effort to shake off her uneasy feeling, she turned and went across to her case, intending to use the time before afternoon tea to unpack.

' . . . *leave* . . . '

This time she was *sure* she heard the word, as clear as crystal. A man's voice, she thought, but little more than a whisper. She turned and faced the room. The *empty* room.

'Who . . . who's there?' she asked, her voice a little higher than it should have been.

There was no reply.

She took a long, slow look around the room, and then — she didn't really know why — she went to the bed and peered beneath it. However unlikely, she hoped for a moment that someone might be playing a practical joke on her, albeit a very *impractical* one. Had the twins been home, she might have suspected that they were having some fun at their new tutor's expense.

But the twins *weren't* at home. And like it or not, she had to accept that the room was empty.

'. . . *Never* . . . *leave* . . . '

Upon hearing the sibilant whisper, she stood up again, her hands folding into nervous fists at her sides. 'Who's there?' she asked, feeling foolish and frightened all at once. And again, this time injecting a little iron into her tone: 'Who's there?' She strained her ears, trying to prepare herself to hear the reply, but there was none.

She searched the room again, thinking that maybe it had been fitted with a speaking tube, but she could find no such appliance. She hurried back to the fire and tried as best she could to look up into the chimney, wondering if by some fluke it might have been a conductor of sound, but again she found nothing to confirm the suspicion.

A log in the fire popped, and she almost jumped out of her skin. *I'm not going mad*, she thought. *I really did hear that voice.* A man's voice. Soft and slow. Like Gerald Averill's, she thought. *Or like his father's.*

Again she waited and listened. Five minutes passed, and then she heard a new sound — a low scratching that came from the other end of the room. She recognized it at once as that of a mouse scurrying along behind the wainscoting, and shuddered.

It's all right, she told herself. *Calm down. There's a perfectly rational explanation for this.*

Which is . . . ?

She had no answer.

Never leave, the voice had said. But just then that was exactly what she wanted to do — to leave and never return!

Still, she couldn't allow herself to do that. Yet again she reminded herself that she had given her word. And so she would make the best of it.

She had no choice.

★ ★ ★

Afternoon tea with Gerald and Leona was no less awkward than her first interview. Leona said little, seeming to be caught up in a world of her own, and neither of them showed particular interest in their twins' education.

'All we ask,' said Gerald, 'is that you furnish them with an understanding of the basics — of English language and literature, of handwriting, mathematics and geography . . . and perhaps the odd nature walk.'

'Certainly,' Meg replied. 'I have found that sewing and needlework are also very popular with girls.'

'Then by all means add that to your curriculum,' Gerald said carelessly.

She sipped at her tea. 'I will need a room where we might hold lessons,' she said after a while.

'We have no shortage of rooms. You may have your pick.'

'Thank you. Oh, and I will need books, if you have them, and perhaps an atlas or two.'

'We have a very comprehensive

library in the drawing room,' he said. 'You may help yourself to whichever volumes you require.' He dabbed at his mouth with a napkin. 'While I think about it, Mrs. Averill and I will be absent tomorrow. We have business to attend to in town and do not expect to return until late afternoon. But I'm sure you will have plenty to occupy you until our return.'

'Indeed.'

She retired early that evening and lay for a while beneath her blankets, enjoying the strangely familiar smell of the room and not wanting to listen to the silence but unable to ignore it. How long before the occasional crackle of the low fire was joined by that soft whispering voice again? But after an hour, she convinced herself that she would not hear it again, and gradually she allowed herself to relax enough to begin to doze.

At the far end of the room, a mouse scuttled along behind the wainscoting.

★ ★ ★

When she entered the dining room the next morning, Angela told her that the master and mistress had already left for town. She heard the news with relief. Perhaps a day to herself would allow her the chance to get used to her new surroundings. In any case, as Gerald had pointed out, she had plenty of other duties to occupy her.

Directly after breakfast she went into the drawing room, and there, under the watchful eyes of the Victorian dolls on the chaise longue, she inspected the books in their display cases. They were mostly old volumes of differing sizes, many in Latin, some in German, yet others in French. Most had such obscure titles as *The History of the Egyptian Religion*, *The Worship of the Romans*, *Natural Law in the Spiritual World*, *Deutsche Mythologie*, *The Light of Egypt* (or, *The Science of the Soul and Stars*), *Supernatural Religion*, the four-volume *Blatter und Bluten* and a very, very old pamphlet entitled *Un Dictionnaire Mytholoqique*.

These were of little use to Meg, and so she continued her search. When she came to an old volume entitled *The Etymology of Names*, she opened the display case and took the book from the shelf. Achlys and Ahriman were unusual names, to say the least, and it occurred to her that she might engage the twins' attention immediately by explaining where they came from.

She took the book to one of the armchairs and sat down, then began to leaf through the yellowing pages. Within moments she had found the first entry she sought: *Achlys is a Goddess of Misery and Sadness. She is the Mist of Death, which falls before the eyes just before the moment of passing. She is described as being pale and thin, constantly weeping, with chattering teeth, long fingernails and shoulders covered with dust.*

Meg looked up from the book, unable to think of a single reason why anyone would want to name their daughter after such a dreadful deity. But perhaps the Averills hadn't realized the true meaning of the name, and chosen it simply for its unusual sound.

Still, it was with an uneasy feeling that she searched through the book until she found an entry for the name Ahriman:

Ahriman is the Middle Persian derivative of 'Angra Mainyu', which means 'devil' or 'evil spirit.' In Persian mythology, Ahriman was the name of the god of death, darkness and destruction, and also the arch-enemy of Ahura Mazda, the highest spirit worshipped in the old Mede and Persian religion, which spread across Asia and predates Christianity.

She closed the book, sorry now that she had ever opened it. Again, she could find no sane reason why the Averills would wish to name their child after a devil or evil spirit, but inevitably the revelation brought to mind all those old rumors about Vincent Averill — how he had been in league with the Devil, and regularly raised the dead. It was nonsense — of course it was — but still it made her shiver. She tried to console herself with the thought that the twins, when she finally got to meet them, would be a just as charming as could be and would in no way reflect their names. How could they?

But it was Gerald and Leona who concerned her most, for who would willingly name their children for death, destruction and —

She stopped suddenly. What had that reference to Achlys said? *The Mist of Death, which falls before the eyes just before the moment of passing.* It was not so much the reference to death that troubled her, but rather that of *mist* . . . such as the ever-present mist that lingered here in this isolated valley. Was that just a coincidence? She was inclined to believe so. But it did little to ease her concerns.

With an effort she pulled herself together, replaced the book on the shelf and quickly inspected the remainder, eventually finding a couple of atlases and some illustrated books on botany and fauna upon which she felt she could base some lessons. She carried the books up to her room and then tried to find one of the servants, intending to ask which room she might use as a classroom. She was reluctant to just explore the house all by herself until she found a suitable space; but when she finally located Angela, the housekeeper reminded her brusquely, 'If the master and mistress said that you should take your pick, then surely that is exactly what you should do.'

With a nod she went back upstairs. The house seemed so enormous, she hardly knew where to begin. She walked to the end of the hallway and stopped at the corner where it turned again to the right. Here a cool breeze flowed past her, and was so noticeable she felt sure someone must have left a window open somewhere close by.

At the far end of the hall there stood a doorless aperture beyond which lay a set of stairs. Quickly trying to get her bearings, she thought it probably led up to the central tower. Curiously, she approached it. As she drew closer, the drop in temperature became even more marked. With a shiver, she looked up the staircase. It rose no more than thirteen steps until it reached a small landing and a single door. Wondering if this was where the window had been left open, she placed one hand on the oak banister before beginning to climb, then drew her hand away quickly. The banister wasn't just cold to the touch, it was positively freezing!

As she rubbed her fingers against her palm to chase away the chill, she tried to think about this logically. If the house had a cold pantry, it would be most likely situated in a north-facing room, and for maximum effectiveness preferably in the cellar. Even if the Averills had fitted an ice house, which they could most certainly afford, it would be separate from the main house, and she certainly had not seen it. It was most likely as she had first suspected — that someone had accidentally left a window open; and in the present cold snap, it wouldn't take long for the entire house to get cold.

Again she started climbing the stairs, noticing now that her breath was beginning to fog before her face. By the time she reached the small landing, there was gooseflesh on the backs of her hands, and she could feel cold air blowing from beneath the door. She was just about to turn the brass handle when she noticed a fine sheen of condensation beading the metal. As she suspected, when she touched the handle lightly with her fingertips, it was icy to the touch.

She took a handkerchief from the sleeve of her gray woolen day dress and wrapped it around the handle, for it seemed so cold she felt there was a very real danger that her skin could stick to the alloy. She turned the handle . . . but the door was locked. Oh, well —

'Never . . . leave . . . '

The whisper was so unexpected that she cried out in surprise. The sound echoed in the confines of the little landing. Heart racing, she wondered if the voice had come from the other side of the door; and trying to ignore her rising alarm, she slowly, carefully, placed one ear against the cold oak.

There was only silence in the room beyond.

She stood back, and though it was hard to do so, fought the urge to flee to the relative warmth and safety of the hallway downstairs. She glanced behind her, to make sure she really was alone, and then said in a whisper of her own, 'Who are you? What is it you want?'

The air was touched by a faint fragrance then; the same familiar, reassuring smell she had noted in her room the day before. For the moment she couldn't identify it, and before she really got the chance, it was gone, leaving her feeling faintly lost and completely baffled as to why she should feel that way.

'Who are you?' she asked again, still keeping her voice low.

There was no reply.

When she was sure there would be no more communication with . . . with *whatever it was* . . . she turned and descended the staircase and returned directly to her room, her thoughts dominated by the strange voice and its equally cryptic message. She was only dimly aware that her entrance had disturbed the mouse that constantly scuttled back and forth behind the wainscoting.

I am not mad, she told herself very deliberately. And yet it was hardly sane to hear voices.

So what was happening to her? What was the answer?

Further thought was interrupted as she once again caught that familiar smell. This time recognition came immediately, and she thought, *Oh, my word* . . .

It was the smell of Golden Scepter, her father's favorite pipe tobacco.

And the voice, though pitched at little more than a whisper . . .

She realized now that it had belonged

to Jacob Warren.

Stunned by the revelation, she quickly sank down onto the edge of the bed before her legs could betray her altogether. Again she asked herself what was happening to her in this house she had been so reluctant to ever see again. But in that very question she thought she found her answer, for it was true — she *had* been reluctant to come back here, and perhaps in her reluctance she had overstretched her nerves and subconsciously looked for some sort of sign that might comfort her. What could have been more natural than that she should imagine her father's voice, telling her to never leave? The very implication of the statement implied that everything would be all right, should she stay. If she was right and that *was* the case, then she felt she should stop worrying about her new situation and just get on with it.

At once she began to feel better. There was nothing to worry about. Deep down she knew it, and had obviously been trying to convince the part of her that still had doubts.

She gave a sigh of relief, amazed at the lengths to which the subconscious could go to alleviate its fears and concerns. It was, she decided, an important lesson learned.

Downstairs, she heard the front door close. She rose from the bed and went to the window just as John Claydon stamped into view below and set about checking the two-horse team rigged to the waiting Clarence coach. She thought he must be going into town on some errand or other, and on impulse wondered if she might dare ask to travel with him. Having been thinking so fondly of her parents, she decided that it would be good for her spirits if she were to see their old cottage again; and once the idea occurred to her, it was impossible to resist.

She hurried downstairs and out into the raw forenoon. For once, the mist had cleared a little to reveal a lowering sky the color of slate. Clearing her throat, she called John's name. He turned toward her, muffled up against the cold, and dipped his head respectfully.

'May I help you, miss?'

'I was wondering . . . are you going into Pendarren, by any chance?'

He hesitated before replying, then nodded.

'May I join you?'

He looked uncomfortable at the request. 'Well . . . '

'It's just that I should like to visit the cottage where I used to live,' she explained.

Still he paused. 'Don't you have work to do?'

'Not until the twins return home.'

He thought about that, and then nodded slowly. 'Oh yes,' he said strangely. 'The twins.'

'May I join you?' she asked again. 'I don't expect you to wait until I'm ready to return. I'll be more than happy to make my own way back.'

'I wouldn't let you do that,' he said

distractedly. Then, but with clear reluctance, 'All right, miss. But wrap up warm. There's snow on the way.'

Her smile was dazzling. 'Thank you!'

She went back up to her room, where she quickly buttoned herself into a fur-trimmed gray coat in Silvertip velour, with Irish bows along each side seam. Her bag came next, and then she hurried back outside again.

John Claydon opened the coach door for her, and she looked up at him and said once again, 'Thank you. I appreciate your kindness.'

He said nothing. Indeed, his expression seemed to turn even sadder than it already was. He closed the door softly behind her, then climbed up onto the exposed seat and cracked his whip above the heads of his two black horses.

Snow began to fall even before they climbed out of the valley and turned onto the road into Pendarren. It swirled past the coach windows and quickly began to gather along the lacquered wooden frames. Dark gray clouds continued to smudge the sky, and if John was right and they were in for a storm, she only hoped it wouldn't hinder their return journey.

Just then the coach seemed to slew a little beneath her, and she thought for a moment that John would decide to turn back, for conditions really were deteriorating very quickly. But the coach continued forward, and Meg reached up to squeeze her fur collar even more tightly to her throat.

Although the snow was rapidly changing the appearance of the countryside around them, she could still recognize enough to know that they were almost upon Serenity Bridge. Another mile, she thought, and they would be in Pendarren. And though this wasn't the best time she could have chosen to visit her old home, she wasn't sorry. Indeed, she was rather cheered by the realization that things were probably going to work out better for her than she had thought, and felt that seeing her old home again was just the thing she needed to counteract the feeling of isolation that seemed so prevalent at Stormview.

Yet again the coach skidded beneath her as the wheels lost their traction, and she thought she heard John Claydon yelling at the horses, but the howling wind had picked up to such an extent by this time that it was difficult to know for sure.

She sat forward, beginning to grow alarmed because the coach was veering drunkenly across the groaning bridge. She definitely heard John crying out to his horses this time. She suspected that the poor creatures were unnerved by the blizzard and refusing to obey his commands. Quickly she lowered one of the windows so that she might look out and make sure that everything was all right.

It wasn't. Even as she poked her head out into the full force of the storm, the coach lurched to a halt and one of the two horses tried to rise up on its hindquarters and paw at the air.

'Get along, there!' cried Claydon, snapping his whip over the animals' heads.

But the next moment, the coach began to roll backwards, following the slight hump of Serenity Bridge, and the horses' fear increased abruptly as they felt themselves being dragged in reverse. Now both of them began to struggle, until all at once there came the snap of splintering wood, and the coach shuddered again. Eyelids fluttering against the tumbling snow, Meg saw the horses racing off toward the village, the shattered shaft to which they were harnessed now bouncing loosely between them.

The coach continued to roll backwards. To halt it, John wrenched on the brake and the wheels immediately locked. But now, as the iron tires slipped and slid on the covering of icy snow, it began to slither sideways toward the edge of the bridge.

There was no time to react to the catastrophe in the making. Within seconds, the coach struck the wooden railings, and the jolt unseated John. With a cry that almost stopped the blood in Meg's veins, he lost his balance, lurched from the driver's seat and went plunging toward the water, arms and legs pinwheeling frantically. He struck the surface with a hard slap, and water exploded around him.

Meg screamed then, the sound curtailed abruptly as the railings gave way and the coach went through them as if they were matchwood.

The vehicle teetered for no more than a heartbeat . . . and then tipped right off the bridge and down into the freezing cold waters of Mare's Tail Beck.

5

The coach didn't take long to fall. It struck the water on its side, and the glass window shattered. Instinctively Meg reared back, crossing her arms over her face to protect it from the razor-sharp splinters. Then icy water began to pour in through the aperture, filling the interior of the coach at an alarming rate.

As Meg felt it rising up over her feet, ankles, calves and knees, she struggled to escape through the already-open window in the other, now *upper*, door, but it was impossible. Not only was the chill water already stealing away all feeling in her legs, it was also soaking into her coat, adding to its weight and making it impossible for her to move.

Gamely she continued to reach up for the window. It remained just out of her reach. But if she could just drag herself up through that, she might stand a chance of getting to the riverbank and relative safety.

Snow drifted down through the window, adding its own chill to her frozen cheeks. Then the coach sank a little deeper, and the waters of Mare's Tail Beck began to spill in from above, trapping her inside.

Now the urge to panic was overwhelming. As the freezing water stole up over her shoulders and around her neck, she tried her best to fight it, drew in a deep breath, released it, took another, released it, took one more, each time trying to stretch and fill her lungs with as much air as possible. And all the while, her coat was absorbing more and more water, growing heavier, restricting her movements, threatening to drag her down.

The water filled her ears and covered her head. It was now impossible to fight the panic. For frantic seconds, she thrashed around blindly. Bubbles of air trickled from her nose and mouth. Then she opened her eyes, saw darkness save for a square of watery daylight impossibly far above her, and again she reached for the coach door. It was still maddeningly unattainable — the coat was waterlogged and movement was next to impossible.

Fumblingly, she tried to unfasten the buttons. The water made them slippery and hard to grasp. The numbing cold rendered her fingers clumsy and almost immobile. Then one button came undone.

One, she thought, clinging desperately to even that small vestige of hope. *I've done one. I can do another.*

But already her lungs were bursting, the cold was making every nerve in her body ache, she was finding it harder and harder to make even the smallest move, and her mind seemed to be dulling, somehow, becoming too tired to work.

And then, with a jolt that threw her entirely off balance, the coach finally settled at the bottom of Mare's Tail Beck.

Her mind screamed for air, told her that she couldn't hold her breath much longer, and that in turn only increased her sense of panic. Thoroughly engulfed by fear, she made one last fumbling attempt to unbutton her coat, but it was no good: the edges of her vision were steadily darkening and she realized that her heart, which by rights should have been pounding, was actually slowing down.

She knew she was going to die . . . that she was going to die a similar death to that of her father in almost exactly the same location. She realized that she could do nothing to fight it . . . nothing to avoid it . . . and so, with incalculable sadness, she surrendered to it.

The coach shook again, bringing her back to some hazy semblance of consciousness. She looked up and saw the silhouette of a man standing on its overturned side, up to his knees in water. A second later he thrust his head under the water and their eyes met. She saw his go wide with surprise, and in some dark recess of her brain she decided that would probably be the last thing she ever saw.

Then blackness swallowed her whole.

She didn't see the man drop urgently to his knees, thrust one arm down through the open window, twist his fingers into the collar of her coat and heave upward with every ounce of strength he had in him.

She saw nothing.

She heard nothing.

She was gone.

* * *

For a long time there was only darkness and silence.

And then . . .

Meg realized dimly that a voice was calling her name, and felt, vaguely, that she should respond to it. It was a male voice, distorted by echoes, and it seemed to be coming from a long way off. She went to take a breath, realized her throat was filled with water, and quickly retched to the side. Hands touched her, squeezed encouragingly, and the voice said, 'That's it. You're all right now, Meg. You're going to be all right.'

She didn't *feel* all right. She felt . . . when she tried to find the right word, she was puzzled. How *did* she feel, exactly? It suddenly occurred to her that she had no idea who she was, *where* she was or what she was doing in this strange black world so full of echoes. Then, slowly, her thoughts began to coalesce, and fragments of what had happened came back to her in little flashes of memory.

She was drowning!

She sat up abruptly, struggling to escape from the confines of the water-filled coach. Immediately strong arms took hold of her again and held her still. The voice — clearer now, no longer as distorted as it had been — said again, 'It's all right, Meg. You're safe now.'

She looked around wildly, still thoroughly baffled. She was beneath some trees beside Mare's Tail Beck, and it was still snowing fiercely. A bicycle had been thrown carelessly against one of the trunks. There was a small fire nearby — someone had built it hastily to help her fight off the bone-deep chill that even now was making her teeth chatter. She was wet through, her hair hanging down over her face like so many rats' tails, and steam was just starting to rise from the drenched material of her coat.

A young man was kneeling over her, as soaking wet as she was. As he looked down at her, she saw water dripping from his short chestnut-brown hair. He looked as chilled as she felt, but his gentle brown eyes were alert as he examined her. 'Are you all right?' he asked.

She nodded. 'I . . . I think so.'

'Can you move your arms and legs?'

'Yes.'

He rubbed her hands briskly. 'Let's get you a little closer to the fire, if we can.'

'John Claydon!' she said abruptly,

and instinctively made to rise.

He quickly held her back, his handsome face darkening. 'Meg — '

'But he fell from the bridge! He went into the water!'

'We're too late,' he told her quietly.

All movement in her ceased then, and she stared at him for a long moment before at last she spoke in a near-whisper, 'He's . . . dead?'

He nodded sadly. 'I rescued you first,' he replied. 'Then went back in to try and find John. I was too late — the current must have dragged him away before I got here.'

She was numb as she thought about that. It was hard to believe that what had started as a simple trip into the village could have ended so tragically. John Claydon . . . She saw his face again in her mind. She had always been so scared of him as a child, and yet he had developed a curious vulnerability over the years, and all she could feel now was sorrow that he should have met such a terrible end.

It also reminded her of her father, and just how close she had come to sharing his fate. And this time when she shivered, it had nothing to do with the biting cold.

He helped her to move closer to the small blaze, and the warmth on her face felt marvelous. 'What . . . happened, exactly?' she asked. 'Everything's still so jumbled up.'

'As near as I can see, John had some trouble with the horses.'

'He did,' she said, remembering.

'And the wagon shaft snapped off. The horses bolted for town — that's how I came to spot them. And the coach . . . I guess it slipped and crashed through the bridge's retaining wall and . . . well, you know the rest.'

Silence, broken only by the blowing wind, settled between them.

'I'm sorry I couldn't do more to get you out of this weather,' he apologized. 'The trees are keeping off the worst of the storm, but even so, we need to get you out of those wet clothes and into something warm and dry before you catch a — '

'Thank you,' she interrupted, her mind still on John Claydon and his unhappy fate. 'You . . . saved my life.'

'You stay right there,' he replied gently. 'I'll find some more branches and build up this fire. When I'm happy that you're safe and warm, I'll go back into town for help.'

For the first time, she noticed his uniform. It was another parallel with her father. 'You're a policeman,' she said almost wonderingly. And she remembered the fleeting glimpse she'd had of the policeman shortly after she'd arrived in Pendarren the day before.

'And you,' he said, 'are Meg Warren.'

She studied him closer. 'You know me?'

'Oh, yes,' he answered a little wistfully. 'But *you've* obviously forgotten *me*.'

She looked at him more carefully. *No*, she thought. *I haven't forgotten you*. There was definitely something familiar about him, but she'd been too distant and distracted to really notice it before . . .

And then she had it, and recognition made her feel even more lightheaded. 'Adam,' she said softly. 'It *is* you, isn't it?'

Adam Eden nodded. 'It's me,' he said. And before he could say any more, it all caught up with her, and she threw herself into his arms and started sobbing.

He reacted instinctively, holding her tight and squeezing her shoulders and telling her that everything was all right now, and she cried even harder then because that was exactly what she wanted to hear, even though she knew it wasn't necessarily true. She was tired and wet, cold and achy, and no matter how ridiculous it might seem to an outsider, she couldn't help but feel responsible for what had happened; that she had somehow cost John Claydon his life.

And yet she was in Adam Eden's

arms, and it was as if time had stood still there, too. She was the nine-year-old girl on the hill overlooking Stormview again, and Adam was that same little boy who had stood over her, looking so fierce and earnest and willing to face any trial if it meant keeping her safe.

'Let it all out,' he whispered soothingly. 'Just let it all out.'

'B . . . but J-John . . . ' she managed.

'It was an accident,' he told her.

'No,' she said, moving back a little so that she could look into his face, a face that was unmistakable to her now; still so beloved, just a little more mature. 'If I hadn't s-stopped him when I did, he might have cr-crossed the bridge safely.'

'I don't understand.'

'I asked h-him to wait for me,' she explained. 'He was going into Pendarren a-and I asked if I could go with him. If he hadn't had to wait for me to g-get my coat . . . '

'You can't think like that, Meg,' he told her without criticism. 'If you want the truth of it, it was just a fluke — a rotten, lousy thing that happened and would have happened no matter what. But it wasn't your doing.'

She looked down into her lap, her thoughts and emotions still all mixed up.

'Where exactly did you spring from, anyway?' he asked to distract her. 'And what on earth were you doing with John Claydon, of all people?'

'He wasn't the way he was when we were children,' she said, feeling that she had to defend him now. 'He was . . . different, somehow. Sad. Broken.'

'I guess that was the drink,' he replied. 'But you haven't answered my question.'

'I'm staying at S-Stormview,' she said.

His expression slackened. '*What?*'

She nodded. 'Y-yes, I know. Storm-view.' She tried to smile but felt her lips quivering again. Despair caught up with her anew and she looked out at Mare's Tail Beck, where the snow was still drifting down onto its wind-rippled surface. 'I lost my job in London, but . . . another one came up, here. I'm to teach Gerald Averill's t-twins.'

He shook his head. 'I didn't even know he had children, much less twins.' He saw her expression and added, 'Yes, they still keep very much to themselves, just as they always did. Go on.'

'There's n-nothing more to tell. I arrived yesterday, but the twins are away, so today I thought I . . . I'd go into the village and . . . look around.'

'Well, you've given me a surprise sooner rather than later,' he said, hoping to raise her spirits. 'After your mother took you away, I never thought I'd see you again.'

'Perhaps it was a mistake to come back.'

'But you did.'

'I felt . . . oh, it's silly, really. I gave my word that I would accept the job . . . but that was before I knew it meant coming back here, and to Stormview, of all places. Do you remember that day we tried to explore it?'

'I'm not likely to forget it.'

Her eyes met his. They were dark and warm, despite the weather, and she knew he was thinking of the connection they'd made that afternoon, on the slope overlooking the house. 'It *did* happen, didn't it?' she said. 'I mean, it wasn't our imagination, was it? Those figures, that chanting, the bell . . . '

'I remember it like it was yesterday,' he said soberly. 'No, it wasn't our imagination.'

'Well . . . having given my word, I didn't like to go back on it. Silly, I know, but my dad always told me to — '

'Your dad,' he interrupted, and now his tone assumed even greater warmth. 'I never really knew my own dad, as you know. He died when I was still just a baby. Perhaps that's why I idolized yours. It's certainly why I went into the police force.'

She would have been touched by the sentiment at any time; but just then, with her emotions so raw, it was almost more than she could handle. 'And you stayed here, in Pendarren,' she managed.

'When I finished my training, the Devon County Constabulary sent me here because I knew the area. It's not as exciting as it would be in a big city like London, of course — well, not normally, at any rate — and I'd love that, but I was happy to come back.' He paused briefly, then said, 'Had John been drinking, do you know?'

She shook her head. 'You don't have to try and make me feel better about it.'

'I'm not. But he *was* a drinker. Maybe you ran into difficulties because he was drunk.'

'He wasn't. At least, not that I could tell.'

'Still . . . he should have known better than to chance the trip in these conditions.'

'The blizzard didn't really start until we were underway.'

'He could have turned back.'

'I thought that. But perhaps he

thought we could make it.' She wasn't comfortable discussing John just then, and changed the subject. 'Where did you come from, anyway?'

'It's as I said. I was doing my rounds when the snow started. I didn't think there was much point in continuing them so I decided to go fort up at the Old George until the worst of it passed. I was just about to do that when the horses came racing down the high street. I saw that they still had a broken shaft between them, and knew someone must be in trouble, so I managed to stop them and then cycled out here to help, if I could.'

'I'm glad you did,' she said in a small voice.

'So am I,' he replied with feeling. 'If I hadn't seen those horses when I did . . .'

There was no need to say more. Because she didn't want to dwell on that, she said, 'Do you still live in the village?'

He nodded. 'When my mother died, I

inherited our cottage.'

'I'm sorry to hear about your mother. She was a lovely woman.'

'Aye, she was. How's *your* mother?'

'She passed away, too,' she said. 'I think she thought it would be easier to get over . . . you know, what happened to my dad . . . if we moved away.'

'And was it?'

'Not really. She never really got over it. She was always listening for footsteps in the street outside, a knock at the door. It was like she was still expecting him to come home. Only . . . '

'Only, what?'

'Oh, nothing.'

'No, go on. I want to know.'

She thought about it for a moment. She had never really tried to articulate it before, and even she was somewhat surprised when she said, 'Only it wasn't so much like she was expecting him to come home. It was more like she was *dreading* it. Isn't that silly?'

He made no reply to that, just looked at her for a long, steady moment. Then:

'I know this is hardly the time or the place,' he said in a low voice, 'but I never forgot you, Meg. I never forgot that day, either. And I certainly never stopped lo — ' He bit off suddenly. 'What's wrong?'

She put one frozen hand to her brow and shook her head. 'I d-don't know . . . I'm f-feeling a little . . . '

Before she could say more, their attention was taken by a growling sound coming from the direction of the bridge. Finding it increasingly impossible to think straight, Meg found herself wondering despairingly what new trial awaited them. Then Adam leapt to his feet and said, 'Stay here.'

He raced out of the trees and into the storm, spraying snow with every stride he took, until she saw him reappear on the bridge. In the meantime, the growling sound continued to build until she caught sight of something red coming out of the snow. Adam planted himself in the center of Serenity Bridge and started to wave his arms back and forth above his head, and a moment later she recognized Gerald Averill's red automobile, the De Dion Bouton, as it came to a spluttering halt.

Adam hurried around the vehicle, spoke urgently, then gestured toward the trees. An instant later Gerald Averill tore a blanket from some sort of compartment behind him, jumped out of the vehicle, and together they ran down off the bridge and back along the bank.

By then, everything had finally caught up with Meg. She began to shiver almost uncontrollably, she felt drowsy, and the world around her began to tip and tilt drunkenly. Gerald's cry — 'Miss Warren!' — brought her back to her senses briefly, and she was startled by the concern she saw on his normally inexpressive countenance.

Without hesitating, he threw the blanket around her shoulders and said, 'Don't worry, my dear, you'll be all right now.' He turned to Adam, and as her eyes closed, she heard him say, 'Help me get her into the Bouton, and then go back to town as fast as you can and fetch a doctor!'

Gerald reached for her, but Adam quickly stepped between them and scooped Meg into his arms. Gerald stared at him a moment, not just in surprise, but with a sudden flash of insight — that there was more going on here than a policeman helping a victim . . . possibly much more.

Dimly now, Meg felt Adam's fingers give her an encouraging squeeze, and then he was striding back through the snow to the automobile, where Leona sat on a seat upholstered in elephant skin, watching with concern that was every bit the mirror of Gerald's. Adam stepped up onto the running board and set Meg down gently on the forward double seat, which faced that reserved for the driver and his companion. It was difficult because the vehicle was small to begin with, and a steering column anchored to the center of the floor and topped with some kind of turning handle cut space down still further.

When he was sure Meg was as comfortable as she could be, Adam stepped back and allowed Gerald to slide in behind the steering apparatus. The master of Stormview worked some of the controls and the automobile sputtered back to life.

'Get that doctor,' Gerald ordered. 'And come back with him yourself. I want to know exactly what happened here.' Then the vehicle rolled down off the bridge and back toward Stormview.

Adam needed no second urging. As exhausted as he himself was, he ran, stumbling, back into the trees, stamped out the fire and then snatched up his bicycle.

6

By the time they reached Stormview, Meg was in a bad way. Gerald carefully lifted the pallid, shivering girl out of the car and carried her inside, calling for Angela as he went.

'Come with me,' he ordered when she finally came scurrying from the kitchen. 'I want you to strip these wet clothes from Miss Warren, dry her off as best you can and then get her into bed.'

Angela's eyes widened at the unexpected request. 'What happened, sir?' she asked, following him up the staircase.

'There was an accident.'

She glanced back toward the still-open front door, where Leona was just letting herself inside. 'Is Mr. Claydon all right, sir?' she enquired.

'He's dead,' Gerald replied bluntly. As Angela processed that, he barked, 'Why was he driving into the village, anyway?'

'I don't know, sir. He just said he had some errands to run.'

'On a day like this?'

'I just assumed . . . '

Not waiting to hear what she assumed, he came to a halt before Meg's bedroom door and waited impatiently for Angela to open it for him. He carried the girl inside, set her down on the bed, then crossed to the fire and quickly began stoking it to life. 'Hurry up, woman,' he snapped when he turned and saw that the housekeeper was still just staring down at Meg.

'Is she going to die?' Angela asked fearfully.

'No,' he replied vehemently. 'No, she is *not* going to die. Do you hear me? She is *not* going to die! I won't permit it!'

*   *   *

The local doctor was an elderly man named Shore. Adam wasted no time in fetching him out to the house. When they arrived in the doctor's little governess cart about thirty minutes later, Leona immediately showed Dr. Shore up to Meg's room. As Adam made to follow him, however, Gerald laid a hand on his arm.

'If you don't mind,' he said, indicating that Adam should precede him into the drawing room, 'I should like a full report on what occurred.'

Adam hesitated. More than anything else just then, he wanted to be with Meg. But he knew there was nothing useful he could do now except wait and pray. Besides, a man had already died. It was not unreasonable that his employer should want to know how it had happened.

Tucking his cap under one arm, he went into the drawing room and Gerald closed the doors behind him. As athletic as he was, Adam was almost dead on his feet. The bicycle ride out to Serenity Bridge in such dreadful conditions had sapped him. His dive into the freezing water and the frantic journey back to Pendarren to fetch the doctor had used up most of his reserves. Added to that, he was still wet through, and chilled to the core.

Gerald must have seen as much, because he gestured Adam toward the fire. He went to a drinks cabinet and poured a stiff brandy, which he handed over. Adam took it with a nod of thanks, and stood for a moment just allowing himself to thaw out.

'It's much as I told you when I first stopped you on the bridge,' he explained. 'As near as I can see, the horses spooked in the storm, the wagon-shaft broke, and the carriage itself slid sideways, smashed through the retaining wall and went right off the bridge.'

'And John died,' Gerald concluded softly.

'It certainly looks that way. According to Miss Warren, he fell from the wagon seat and hit the water with quite a force. It probably knocked him senseless, he sank and . . . ' His voice trailed off, he took a quick reviving nip at the brandy and finished with, 'It was a rotten business all round.'

'But thanks to your quick response, Miss Warren was saved.'

He nodded. 'Talking of Meg, sir, how was she when you got her here?'

'Chilled to the bone, unconscious. I pray that it is nothing more than reaction.'

'So do I.'

The comment, and the heartfelt way in which it was delivered, gave Gerald the opening he had been seeking. 'I note that you referred to Miss Warren by her first name,' he remarked, his tone elaborately casual. 'Do I take it that you know her?'

Adam nodded. 'We grew up together.'

'I thought it was something like that. You seemed exceptionally . . . concerned . . . for her welfare.'

'I'd feel that way about anyone in her situation, Mr. Averill.'

'Did you know she was coming here?'

'No, sir.'

'She didn't write ahead to tell you?'

'No, sir. There was no reason why she should — we lost touch years ago. It was a complete surprise to me when I dragged her out of the carriage and recognized her.'

'Then there is nothing between the two of you?'

Adam frowned. 'I don't quite follow you, Mr. Averill.'

'Then allow me speak frankly, Constable. I make it a rule — a rule I have always strictly enforced — that no one in my employ should have followers or suitors. And you *would* like to be her suitor, wouldn't you?'

'I — '

'Before you deny it,' said Gerald, 'it's written all over your face.'

Adam said mildly, 'With the greatest respect, Mr. Averill, my intentions toward Miss Warren — assuming I *have* any — are none of your business.'

'On the contrary — they are very much my business. Miss Warren is here to teach my children. As such, I have to satisfy myself that she sets the best possible example to them.'

'I can understand that,' said Adam, feeling an uncharacteristic anger rising in him and cautioning himself to remain calm. 'Nevertheless, she is entitled to a life beyond teaching. And you'll have to forgive me, sir — I'm afraid I didn't even know you *had* children.'

Gerald gave a bitter smile, then went to the window, there to watch the snow still falling. Without turning back to Adam, he said, 'We — that is, my wife and I — keep largely to ourselves. We do this because we follow certain religious beliefs, and wish to avoid ridicule and condemnation by those who would seek to judge us. As a consequence, we are more comfortable among our own kind, and thus do not go out of our way to fraternize, or share details of our life, with what we would call 'outsiders'. That in itself inspires a degree of suspicion and dislike, as I am sure you are already aware, but we have learned to live with that.'

He turned back again. 'Now, I see no reason why Miss Warren should not be perfectly happy here. She came with excellent references, and from what I have already seen, she will be more than equal to the task ahead of her. But I repeat — no member of staff is allowed any followers, or any suitors. So I would suggest that you forget whatever romantic dalliance you might have entertained, if not out of respect for my family and me, then most certainly out of respect for Miss Warren.'

Adam set his glass down on the mantelpiece. 'I can assure you, Mr. Averill, that I have the utmost respect for Miss Warren, and always have done. And were I to consider any form of relationship with her — assuming she would be willing to entertain one — it could never be termed a 'dalliance', and I very much resent the implication that it might. Now, at the moment we are agreed that Miss Warren's health is our primary concern. What happens after that, if anything, will certainly not impact upon her work or her responsibilities to your children.'

Gerald's features tensed. 'I must remind you that you are a public servant, Constable. I expect you to behave like one, especially while you are under my roof.'

'I *am* a public servant,' Adam agreed readily. 'But I am not *your* servant, Mr. Averill. You are free to pass any comment you wish upon my professional conduct, but you have no right whatsoever to tell me what I can and cannot do in my personal life. And while I respect your religious beliefs, you have no right to impose them on Miss Warren.'

Gerald's eyes lidded dangerously. 'I am not without influence in this region,' he said softly. 'And as such I can be a very good friend, or a very bad enemy, depending upon how I am treated. You have, I am certain, a promising career ahead of you. If you value it, you will make sure that I remain a friend.'

'I don't believe I like the sound of that,' said Adam, positively bristling now. 'It sounds very close to a threat.'

'You may take it whichever way you choose. I would call it advice — *good* advice.'

But Adam had heard enough. And though he made an effort to contain his growing anger, he could contain it no longer. Before he could stop himself, he said, 'Had I not been raised so well, Mr. Averill, I think I would tell you what to *do* with your advice.'

Gerald blinked in astonishment at such impertinence, and his own anger spilled over. 'Very well,' he grated. 'I have tried to be reasonable about this. Now I see I shall have to — '

Without warning, the door opened and Leona ushered Dr. Shore into the room. An electric silence immediately descended.

The doctor was in his late sixties, with a round, pale face and thinning white hair. He and Leona came to a sudden halt side by side, each aware that they had inadvertently barged in on some kind of argument. Gerald recovered first and asked, 'How is she, Doctor?'

'She has suffered a severe shock,' Shore replied, studying him over a pair of delicate pince-nez. 'And little wonder. Not only did she come close to drowning, but she also, I believe, witnessed the death of your man, John Claydon.'

'Will she be all right?' asked Adam.

'Don't look so worried, lad,' the doctor answered with a smile. 'She underwent a process called vasoconstriction, that's all.'

'Vaso . . . ?'

'At times of great stress,' Shore explained patiently, 'the body's blood vessels narrow in order to conserve the flow of blood to the vital organs. The trouble is, the body also releases a chemical known as adrenaline at the same time, and when this happens, it can sometimes cause a drop in blood pressure. Put simply — she fainted.'

Gerald snorted. 'Is that *all*?'

'It is not as trivial as it might sound,' admonished the doctor. 'Barring any unforeseen complication, Miss Warren should be fine. She is young, and she is strong. And if she's anything like her father, whom I was privileged to know, she'll be a fighter. But still, we must watch her carefully for the next twenty-four to forty-eight hours. It is possible she may suffer nothing more than a cough and a cold. But equally, she may develop pneumonia. If she shows any sign of fever, of a fever that alternates with bouts of shivering, or shortness of breath, or a cough that produces blood in the sputum, call me immediately.'

Gerald's shoulders slumped with relief. 'Thank you, Doctor,' he said sincerely. 'And thank you for coming so quickly and in such ghastly conditions. Send me your bill as soon as you like, and I shall attend to it immediately.'

'I will,' replied the doctor. 'Now, if you will excuse me, I'll just collect my bag and be on my way. Are you coming back with me, young Adam?'

Adam nodded. 'Aye. I still need to reclaim the coach, and find some men to help me drag the beck for poor John Claydon's body.'

But Gerald stayed him with a gesture and said hurriedly, 'Before you go, I should, ah . . . like one more word — in private.'

Dr. Shore looked from one to the other. Leona, too, regarded them both with open curiosity. Then, finally understanding the part she must play, she nodded and said, 'Come this way, Doctor. I'm sure you would like a cup of hot, strong tea to fortify you before you brave this weather again.'

She led him from the room and closed the doors softly behind her. When they were alone again, Gerald said somewhat awkwardly, 'I would like you to know that I very much regret our earlier exchange, Constable Eden. Though it is no excuse, I can only blame my momentary lapse in manners upon my concern for Miss Warren's welfare. I rather suspect that we may ascribe your own behavior, too, to a similar cause.'

Startled by the other's unexpected show of contrition, Adam said readily, 'We may, sir.'

'Good,' said Gerald, offering his hand. 'Then you will accept my apology, and we'll say no more about it.'

They shook.

'Now, I am sure you would like to see Miss Warren before you leave, if only to satisfy yourself that all is well with her. But you will understand that I cannot rescind my rule regarding followers and suitors.'

Without waiting for a response, he led the way across the room and out into the hallway. Adam followed him as they ascended the stairs. The echoes they sent up to the rafters multiplied until they sounded like thunder, and he thought that he had never known such a dark and uninviting house. No wonder Stormview still held a morbid fascination for the villagers, even after all these years — the place itself was so bizarre, its occupants so strange and secretive.

Then Gerald knocked softly at Meg's bedroom door, and a few seconds later it was opened by Angela. 'She's sleeping, sir,' the housekeeper reported as they went inside.

The room was as warm as toast, but still Adam was shocked by how pale Meg's skin looked, especially in contrast to her long auburn hair, which was fanned out on the pillow beneath her. He slowly went forward, no longer aware of Gerald or the housekeeper. All that existed for him — all that had *ever* existed for him, he finally acknowledged to himself — was Meg.

He watched the counterpane rise and fall steadily in time with her breathing, saw her features twitch a little and then relax, and wondered what she was seeing in her deep, troubled sleep.

Meg . . .

Nothing would have given him

greater pleasure than to call upon her when she was fully recovered. He had always felt an affinity with her, a connection that always seemed to have been there. And when her mother had taken her away to London so abruptly, his life had never been quite the same. The boy had grown into a man, and the man had encountered other girls in the course of his life, but none of them had ever attracted him as she had.

But he had no wish to ruin her chances of employment here, and no right to assume that she might still feel that same unique bond with him. And for that reason he knew he must leave her in peace and do nothing to jeopardize her position at Stormview.

'As you can see,' Gerald said, coming up behind him, 'she is being given every care, and I have no doubt that she will recover her health very shortly. I will send word immediately when this happens.'

Adam turned and nodded. Clearing his throat a little, he said, 'Thank you,

Mr. Averill. I would appreciate that.'

Behind him, Meg's fingers clenched and unclenched fleetingly, and once again her features gave that troubled twitch.

* * *

Gerald stood in the doorway and watched the little governess cart disappear into the snow. As soon as it was out of sight, he went back inside, slammed the door behind him and stormed into the drawing room. Leona, he saw at once, was down on her knees, fussing with the children. He looked at her, at *them*, and an expression of distaste crossed his face.

When she looked up at him, he said, 'I shan't be long.'

The skin at the bridge of her nose pinched a little. 'You're going somewhere?'

'Into Pendarren. I have to send a telegram.'

The children forgotten, she came to

stand before him. 'What's wrong?' she asked.

His lips curled. '*Everything*. That policeman — he knows her. Worse, he's *besotted* with her. So I'm sending for Dr. Valentine.'

A shiver ran through her. 'I hate that man,' she said, and pouted just like a child herself.

'Nevertheless, he has his uses.'

'But Dr. Shore . . . he said she would be fine,' she said after a moment. 'Do you not trust his judgment?'

'I'm not calling on Valentine for the girl's sake,' he explained irritably. 'I need him to take care of the policeman.'

He watched as she tried to understand his meaning. Inevitably, she failed. But he had grown used to the woman she had become, the one who sometimes struggled with the simplest thing, whose mind was ever in a constant state of preoccupation. 'Is that necessary?' she finally asked.

As patiently as he could manage, he

said, 'It is crucial that no one knows she is here — at least no one who is likely to ask questions after she disappears. That policeman *will* ask questions, because he loves her. I could see it when I looked into his eyes.'

'How romantic,' she said wistfully.

'When she vanishes, he will want to know where she's gone and why — which makes him an unforeseen complication . . . though, fortunately, one we can eliminate.'

She was still thinking about what he had said. He could almost see the workings of her mind in her expression. For an instant he wondered why he had ever married her to begin with. But then, he remembered that she had been a different woman when they had first met — lively, quick-witted, ambitious. She had been ready to try any thrill, no matter how perverse, so that she might experience life, and everything it had to offer, to the full. And as such, she had been his perfect companion.

But then, when he felt she could be

trusted, when he felt she was ready for it, he had introduced her to the ultimate experience. Only, the ultimate experience had proved too much for her mind to accept, much less embrace. He had not anticipated that. He had not anticipated that she would fall apart emotionally; that the sights she had witnessed that night would leave her unhinged and unable ever to return to full sanity.

And so he humored her, he tolerated her, he allowed her the indulgence of her precious children, and deep inside he despised her for what she had become, and despised himself for still loving her too much to consign her to an institution and be done with it.

'I shan't be long,' he said again, and turned to the door.

Understanding as much as she could of the situation, Leona nodded, and turning back to the children said brightly, 'Say goodbye to Daddy.'

Gerald left the room without looking back.

7

Without warning, Meg snapped awake and lay in the darkness with a pounding heart. Around her, the room was silent but for the sound of her panicked breathing and the busy scurrying of the mouse behind the wainscoting. The low flames in the hearth sent shadows capering across the walls and ceiling, and in her slightly bewildered state she thought they resembled restless ghosts.

For a few seconds more she lay neither fully awake nor fully asleep. But gradually the sounds and images that had haunted her uneasy slumber began to fade — the mournful tolling of a single bell, the low, ominous chanting of figures dressed in cowls and habits, and every so often her father's unmistakable voice telling her to ' . . . *never leave . . .* '

Little by little, her senses began to

return, and the unsettling sounds grew fainter until they finally died away altogether. Instinctively she knew she had been asleep for hours, and yet she still felt exhausted. She wondered why that should be, and for several moments tried to remember where she was and how she'd got there.

A soft moan escaped her when she finally remembered that John Claydon was dead. It was, as Adam had told her, silly to blame herself for John's death, but she couldn't help it. If she hadn't delayed him at the last moment by asking if she might accompany him into Pendarren, things might have turned out much differently for him.

The blame she placed upon herself made her feel wretched. But physically, she realized that she felt much better than she had any right to, considering what she'd been through. When she sat up, her limbs felt heavy and achy; but apart from that and the tiredness, her breathing was easy and her mind was, even now, rapidly clearing.

She had Adam to thank for her life. Adam, who had always been there for her. And as she thought of him, his even-featured face so chilled by the weather, his chestnut hair darkened by the waters of the beck, the concern in his chocolate-brown eyes so genuine, she understood that she had never really stopped loving him, merely resigned herself — reluctantly — to never seeing him again.

When her mind had cleared sufficiently for her to recognize him again, she had seen immediately that he was still as sincere as he had always been, serious when he needed to be, still able to crack a joke and smile so wide when the occasion demanded it. Then she recalled what he had said just before Gerald and Leona had come along in their automobile, and it sent a strange thrill coursing through her.

I never forgot you, Meg. I never forgot that day, either. And I certainly never stopped lo —

Had he been about to say what she

thought he'd been about to say? Surely not, after so many years. But what if he had always felt the same way she did?

Then:

' . . . *leave . . . never . . . leave . . .* '

She stiffened and looked around the room, for the voice seemed to come at her from everywhere at once.

The room, of course, was empty. But now she was thoroughly puzzled. She believed she had explained away her father's voice as nothing more than a manifestation of her subconscious; that in essence, she had been trying to convince herself that everything would be all right for her here at Stormview. And that explanation had certainly made sense. So why should she hear the voice again, now? And why those same, cryptic words?

'Dad?' she called uncertainly.

The mouse scampered back the other way along the wall.

'*Dad?*' she whispered again.

Nothing.

'I'm all right, Dad, if that's what

you're worried about,' she told the darkness. 'I'll be all right, here.'

But there was only silence, until . . .

There came a sudden, faint click of sound, and she snapped her head around in time to see the bedroom door open just a fraction. She waited, expecting someone to come in, perhaps to check on her. But no one did.

' . . . *look* . . . ' whispered her father's voice.

She frowned, and began to wonder if everything she had been through had affected her mind, and that this was all just in her imagination, a product of some delirium. But it seemed too real to dismiss so easily. And the door *had* just clicked open — there was no imaging that.

' . . . *look* . . . ' said the voice again, and without really understanding how, she got the distinct impression that it wanted her to leave the room; that it wanted to show her something.

She pushed back the covers and sat up. Her muslin nightdress rustled softly

143

in the darkness. She stood up slowly, carefully, but her balance was fine. With a shiver, she went barefoot to the dresser, upon which sat a brass twin-burner oil lamp, and quickly struck a match to light it. At once, the darkness retreated. She carried the lamp back to the bedside stand, where there sat a mahogany balloon clock. It was almost two o'clock in the morning.

' . . . *look* . . . ' the voice whispered again.

Lamp in hand, she went to the door and, summoning all her courage, pulled it open. The lamp threw a limited circle of light out into the paneled hallway beyond. She stepped across the threshold and looked to the left, then the right. Around her, Stormview was silent, asleep. Feeling both foolish and just a bit apprehensive, she whispered, 'What is it you want me to see, Dad?'

There came no immediate response. But all at once a stray draught sprang up as if from nowhere, stirred the folds of her nightdress and made the lamp flicker, and send the shadows yawing toward the far end of the hallway.

Eyes wide and unblinking, breathing shallowly now, she turned in that direction, knowing without knowing how that the voice wanted her to retrace her steps to that doorless aperture at the end of the second hallway, beyond which lay the staircase that led to the ice-cold central tower.

Instinctively she wanted to ignore the direction, to return to her room and close and lock the door and wait for the sun to rise. Perhaps she was being wholly irrational, but she sensed that there was something inside that tower that she would rather not see.

But again she made an attempt to overcome her fears. And almost before she realized it, she was following the hallway around the corner to where the doorless aperture waited at its far end like the open maw of some hungry creature.

Stop it! she cautioned herself. *You're a sensible, rational girl, and you shouldn't let your imagination get the better of you.* But that was easier said than done.

At last she found herself standing right before the gap, beyond which lay thirteen stairs and a door with a brass knob that was like ice to the touch.

Chill bumps rose on her arms, for the air here was still as cold as it had been yesterday morning, and likely to get even colder as she ascended the stairs to the locked door. Nevertheless, she slowly began to climb, conscious of every soft groan and creak the treads made beneath her. And in the lamplight, she saw her breath misting and thought bleakly, *This isn't my imagination, either.*

Then she was on the little landing, and the door into the tower stood before her like an invitation she would rather not have received. Cautiously she put her ear to the cold door. She heard nothing but the overloud rasp of her own anxious breathing. She stepped back again, swallowed nervously, then reached for the brass door handle. It was, as she had expected, bitingly cold to the touch. But this time, when she turned the handle, the door opened softly.

A wave of cold air rushed out to meet her and she shivered, the breath clouding even more noticeably before her face. Hesitantly, she pushed the door wide and went inside.

The lamp struggled to light the room beyond a few feet. It was as if the darkness refused to be banished by the light. But as near as she could see, she was in an empty room that looked as if it had once been some sort of chapel. Heavy black velvet drapes hung at the windows — three windows in each of three walls, and four in the fourth.

Thirteen in all, she thought unexpectedly.

And there, directly ahead of her on the far side of the room, stood an altar draped with a red velvet cover. Upon the altar sat a large gold cross, easily two feet high. She felt that the symbol should offer her some much-needed comfort, and ease her growing anxiety. But . . .

But *this* cross was upside down.

Her eyes narrowed as she tried to make sense of it. Had it been left that way by accident? Or was there something more to it, something more symbolic, something . . . blasphemous?

Slowly she went forward until she felt something brush against her face. With a small cry of alarm, she reared back. Had she walked into a spider's web?

Regaining her composure, she lifted the lamp a little higher and saw a length of stout rope hanging from the shadowed rafters. Cautiously she reached out and touched it. Like the rest of the room, it was unnaturally cold. But even as she disturbed the rope, she sensed movement in the darkness above, and there came a soft, metallic chime of sound.

The bell! she thought. The bell she and Adam and the others had heard tolling that day all those years before.

She skirted the rope and continued toward the altar. As she drew closer, light from the lamp reflected off the upside-down cross and also off of something that had been placed directly in front of it, which she hadn't noticed before. She grimaced as she recognized a long knife in a black sheath inlaid with various pewter shapes and figures.

Setting the lamp down on the altar, she reached for and picked up the knife. It slid easily from the sheath. She saw that it had a long double-edged steel blade and a handle that seemed to have been fashioned from onyx, or something very much like it.

She slid the blade back into the sheath and examined the pewter shapes and figures with which it had been decorated. She recognized a triangle within a circle, what seemed to resemble hieroglyphics, an eye complete with brow and what looked like some sort of tail growing from it, and an open hand with a black circle where the palm should be.

This is not good, she told herself worriedly. *This is not right*.

She replaced the knife where she had found it, picked up the lamp and turned, intending to leave this chapel that was in reality no such thing; but then abruptly froze as she noticed, for the first time, the floor across which she had just walked. It had been fashioned from black tiles into which had been worked a large white circle encompassing two stylized triangles, which together formed a five-pointed star.

She recognized it at once as a pentagram. A symbol of evil.

Was this what the voice — her father — had wanted to show her? If so, then surely it was a warning to leave, as opposed to *never* leave.

Whatever it was supposed to mean, she had seen enough — indeed, more than enough. She hurried from the room, closed the door softly behind her, and then returned to her bedroom, there to await the dawn.

* * *

She thought it would never arrive.

Upon returning to her room, she had hastily washed and dressed and packed her belongings. Whether she had given her word or not, she now felt that she could no longer stay at Stormview, not having been into the tower room and seen what it contained. She knew there would be an unpleasant scene as she resigned from a job she hadn't even had a chance to begin. That was unavoidable. But she hoped that the Averills would understand her position and allow her to leave at once. After that . . .

She thought she would try to find lodgings in Pendarren for the time being, and perhaps write to Mrs. Hewitt and explain that the job hadn't worked out. It might even be possible for her to return to St Nicholas's on a part-time basis until funds could be found to employ her more permanently.

One thing, however, was beyond doubt. It had been a mistake to return to Stormview. The only benefit had been to meet Adam again, and even the thought of him just then provided a much-needed comfort, and somehow made the long wait for sunrise more bearable.

At last the window began to lighten, and she went to it, drew back the curtain and looked out into the valley. As she had expected, a thin sulfurous mist drifted lazily just beyond the window, but at least it had stopped snowing, and the countryside — what she could see of it — was painted pristine white.

She glanced at the clock. It was just after five. Three hours had somehow managed to pass more like three months. She briefly considered leaving here and now, and writing a letter of apology for her sudden departure when she was safely away from the house. But somehow she couldn't bring herself to do that. Apart from anything else, she knew she wouldn't get far on foot, not in these inclement conditions, even supposing she could leave without being seen and stopped first. So she continued to wait, and somehow the hands of the clock gradually signaled six o'clock, then seven.

It was then that she heard the front door close, and hurried back to the window. Below, Gerald came into sight, dressed sensibly against the weather in a lamb's-wool overcoat and a homburg hat. He disappeared around the side of the house and shortly thereafter she heard the sound of the automobile's engine roaring to life.

Disappointment washed through her then, as she realized that, had she not decided to wait as long as she had, it might have been possible for Gerald to take her into Pendarren all the sooner, on his way to wherever he was going. A few seconds passed, and then the red De Dion Bouton appeared, and followed the uneven track away from the house until it was eventually lost to sight.

Well, she thought, trying to make the

best of things, *perhaps it will be easier to deal with Leona by herself than both of them together*. And making up her mind to finally make her move, she went toward the door just as it opened and Angela peered inside.

The housekeeper looked surprised to see her up and dressed. She came inside and said brusquely, 'You should still be in bed. Why, just yesterday we all thought you might die.'

'I feel fine today, honestly,' Meg replied, feeling obliged to apologize for her quick recovery. 'And thank you for your concern.'

Angela shrugged. She seemed uncomfortable with any show of appreciation or gratitude. Perhaps she had worked at Stormview so long that she simply wasn't used to it. 'The master told me to look after you, and I did, as best I could,' she said.

'Well, I appreciate it,' said Meg. And then, hesitantly, 'I . . . I've decided to leave.'

Angela scowled at her. 'You've only

just arrived,' she pointed out.

'Yes, I know, but . . . I just don't think the job is really for me.'

The housekeeper's lips thinned. 'Well, the master won't be best pleased.'

'No . . . and I'm truly sorry for that. But . . . perhaps Mrs. Averill will be more understanding.'

Angela snorted. 'I daresay she will,' she allowed. 'But she'll do nothing without the master's approval, if that's what you're hoping for. If you want to be released from your duties here — duties you haven't even taken *up* yet, by the way — it's the master you'll have to speak with, not the mistress.'

'Even so, I *will* speak to Mrs. Averill.'

'Then you had best wait until she rises.'

Meg nodded. 'When will that be?'

'The mistress usually takes breakfast at eight.'

Eight. Meg nodded. Only another hour to wait, then. 'Thank you, Angela.'

Once again, the housekeeper waved her gratitude aside. 'You'll be wanting breakfast yourself, I daresay?'

'Not really. I'm not hungry.'

'Suit yourself,' said Angela shortly. 'But you really ought to keep your strength up as best you can, after what you went through yesterday.'

She turned and let herself out. Meg looked at the door for a long time after it had closed. On the surface, at least, it did seem ridiculous that she should wish to leave so soon after she'd arrived, but perhaps Angela had no idea what lay in the tower room. Certainly she had no problems working here. But then, she had probably never heard that sinister chanting, or the tolling of the bell — or indeed, of a phantom voice issuing its puzzling message.

Her thoughts were interrupted by the sound of the mouse scuttling along behind the wainscoting. A brief, sad smile touched her mouth as she thought, *You know, you're the only thing I will miss about Stormview.*

★ ★ ★

A little after eight o'clock, Meg left her room and went downstairs. On her way toward the kitchen, Angela heard her descending the stairs, and glancing up at her, said gruffly, 'The mistress is in the drawing room, if you want to see her.'

Meg was about to thank her, but Angela was already hurrying on her way.

With butterflies in her stomach, she went to the drawing room, knocked and then opened the double doors. Leona was standing before the window, looking out onto the new misty day. She turned when Meg cleared her throat and said, 'Goodness, you're up and about! Are you sure that's wise, Miss Warren?'

Meg closed the doors behind her. 'I'm very much better, thank you. And thank you for all the care I was given after . . . after what happened yesterday.'

Leona smiled a little vacantly. 'We couldn't let anything happen to you, could we?'

'I also feel responsible for what

happened to Mr. Claydon,' Meg continued. 'Perhaps I shouldn't, but had I not
delayed him as he was about to leave
for Pendarren . . . '

'You cannot fight against fate, Miss
Warren,' Leona pointed out, and all at
once she gave Meg a sudden, direct,
intense look. 'That is something you
would do well to remember.'

Meg nodded politely. 'Be that as it
may, I do regret any part I might have
played, however indirectly, in Mr.
Claydon's death. And that is one of the
reasons I think it would be better if I
relinquished my role here as your
children's governess and allowed some-
body more qualified to take up the
position.'

Leona stared at her, dumbstruck.
Around them, it grew quiet enough to
hear the ticking of the grandfather
clock.

'No,' Leona said at length. 'No.
Gerald would never allow that.'

'Nevertheless, my mind is made up,'
Meg insisted. 'I can only apologize for

the inconvenience I've caused — '

'You don't understand,' said Leona, flustered now. 'You are the only one we want. Nobody else would *do*.'

'I'm sure there are many better-qualified — '

'No,' Leona said again, more firmly this time. 'You *can't* go.' She paused for a moment, as if trying to find an excuse, something to justify her statement. At last a light came into her eyes and she said brightly, 'It's your birthday! We have to mark the occasion.'

Meg blinked. Her birthday — what with one thing and another, she'd forgotten all about that. 'There's really no need,' she protested.

'But — '

'I'd sooner not.'

'Well . . . ' Leona thought some more. Then: 'What about the children? They'll be so disappointed if you leave us.'

Distinctly uncomfortable now, Meg said, 'With respect, Mrs. Averill, the children haven't even *met* me yet.'

'But they have,' Leona returned brightly. 'They saw you the very first day you arrived. But they're shy. They're always shy until they get to know a person.'

'I was . . . under the impression they were staying with relatives,' Meg said carefully.

Leona waved that aside. 'That was just a little white lie,' she answered. 'Wasn't it, children?' And she turned and addressed herself to all the old Victorian dolls on the chaise longue.

As Meg followed her gaze, she felt her skin begin to crawl. Not sure if this was Leona's idea of a joke, she said cautiously, '*These* are your children?'

Leona nodded enthusiastically and crossed toward them. 'Of course,' she said, displaying great animation now, for this was clearly her favorite subject, 'most of them are still too young to require a governess, but I do think Achlys and Ahriman are now ready to begin their studies.' She brushed her fingertips fondly across the heads of two identical dolls.

Without being aware of it, Meg began to back away from her. 'I'm sorry, Mrs. Averill,' she said, and there was no way to hide the tremor in her voice. 'But I have to leave. Now.'

She turned and started for the doors even as they opened and Gerald stood framed in the entrance, still clad in his lamb's-wool overcoat, with hat in hand and melting snow dampening his boots. She halted abruptly as the master of Stormview slowly looked from her to Leona, from Leona to the dolls, and then, finally, back to Meg herself.

'I . . . I was just telling Mrs. Averill,' Meg said. 'I'm afraid I have decided to leave.'

Gerald stared at her for another long moment, his angular face unreadable. Then, at last, he came into the room and closed the doors softly behind him.

'I'm afraid that won't be possible, Miss Warren,' he said softly.

'But — '

'Hush!' he snapped. And then: 'You are never going to leave Stormview ever *again.*'

8

His fingers digging into Meg's arm, Gerald pushed her roughly across the hallway and then started dragging her up the staircase and back to her room.

'What are you doing?' she demanded, struggling against him. 'I told you I wanted to leave!'

'And I told you that you are staying here,' rasped Gerald.

Try as she might, Meg could make no sense out of the dark course events had just taken. 'Look,' she said, trying to placate him, ' . . . if . . . if this is all about Mrs. Averill and those dolls, I promise you I won't say a word!'

'Mrs. Averill is ill,' he said as he continued to climb and drew her along with him. 'She witnessed something a few years ago for which her brain was not prepared, and it left her as you see her today, with a grasp upon reality that is tenuous to say the least. It was always her dearest wish to have children, but after she lost her faculties, I did not think she would be in any fit condition to care for them. However, I allowed her to care for her dolls, which she considers to *be* children.'

'And for that you have my understanding, But — '

'I neither want nor need your understanding, Miss Warren.'

'But if you're afraid that I'll tell anyone, or complain that I was brought here under false pretences ... I understand that you were only trying to humor your wife.'

He stopped suddenly and turned on her. 'You understand nothing,' he said scathingly. 'But you will, Miss Warren. In very short order, now, you will.'

They reached the head of the stairs and, hoping to catch him by surprise, she once again tried to pull away from him. This time he yanked her toward him and, with a curse, slapped her. She stared up at him, and the tears that sprang to her eyes were as much to do with anger as they were to do with pain.

'Let me go,' she breathed.

Ignoring her, he continued to drag her along the hallway.

'What are you going to do to me?' she demanded, feeling somehow obliged to ask the question, but dreading the answer.

'What I have waited *years* to do,' he said.

At last they reached her bedroom door. He opened it and flung her inside. She stumbled, almost lost her balance, then righted herself. She stared at him as he helped himself to the key in the lock.

'I don't understand,' she said, a catch in her voice. 'Keeping me here against my will . . . that's kidnapping, Mr. Averill! When the police find out — '

'They *won't* find out,' he said, and smiled.

'Adam will,' she predicted defiantly.

He was about to close and lock the door, effectively imprisoning her; but before he did, he looked at her one final time and smiled coolly. 'The only thing Constable Eden is likely to discover,' he said, 'is whether he is bound for heaven or hell. Indeed — ' And here he fished out his pocket watch and consulted it briefly. ' — if all has gone according to plan, I rather suspect that he is already bound for one place or the other.'

★ ★ ★

Upon his return to Pendarren the previous day, Adam had rounded up some volunteers from The Old George, commandeered some chains, hooks, ropes and two strong draft horses, and gone back out to Serenity Bridge. There, in foul weather, he had overseen the reclamation of the Averill carriage.

They had left the ruined vehicle on the bank until he could arrange to have it towed to the nearest blacksmith's.

Then had come the part he had been dreading — dragging the beck for John

Claydon's body. It had been a gruesome, ultimately fruitless business, but the men had stuck with it for two miles in each direction until it became obvious that the current had washed the body beyond their reach, or that it had snagged on something in a deep trench they hadn't been able to reach with their hook-tipped ropes.

By the time he returned to the little cottage in which he had grown up, he felt tired and dispirited. He hated the idea that John Claydon's body might remain undiscovered, for though he had been a strange antisocial man, the least he deserved was a Christian burial.

Between jaw-cracking yawns, he had written up a full report of the tragedy, which he would send to his superiors in Exeter the following morning. Then he flopped into an armchair before the roaring fire, and at last allowed the heat to chase the chills from his body.

It was ironic that his reunion with Meg Warren should be overshadowed by such terrible events. And his joy at meeting her again after so many years had been tempered by the knowledge that he must keep his distance if she, in turn, were to keep her job. In any case, he reminded himself, it had been the better part of ten years since they'd seen each other. In that time she had seen much of life beyond the confines of this isolated little village, and would doubtless want more from any relationship than anything a mere bobby on the beat could offer her.

Still . . . seeing her again had brought back just how much she had always meant to him. For as long as he could remember, he had always been drawn to her; and though she had never really needed it, he had always seen himself as her protector. He had been too young then to know that it was love; that realization had only come the day they'd explored Stormview, and it had left him faintly astonished.

After a time he had dozed off in the chair, and woke with a start at two in the morning. Not knowing what had woken him so suddenly, his thoughts immediately returned to Meg. He could only hope she was sleeping soundly just then, and regaining her strength by the minute. He briefly considered going to bed, but decided it wasn't worth it. He leaned forward and used a poker to stir the fire back to life, then sat back again, closed his eyes and gradually drifted off to sleep.

The next time he awoke, it was about half-past six, and when he stood up he had to do so warily, for his neck and back were stiff from sleeping in such an awkward position. He made himself a cup of tea and cooked a quick breakfast, then turned his attention to the day's duties. He would have to get his report off to headquarters, and see to the removal of the Averill carriage. Then he would go up to Stormview to give Gerald a report on his search for John Claydon, and enquire after Meg. With any luck, he might even be allowed to see her again. In fact, he decided to insist upon it.

He was just reaching for his greatcoat when there came a brisk rapping at the cottage door. It was unusual to have visitors at such an early hour, and he wondered if someone might be bringing news of Meg . . . or John.

Leaving his coat where it was, he hurried to answer the summons. A tall, spare-looking man in a long single-breasted morning coat and a silk top hat was standing on the step. He carried a Malacca cane in one hand, a small black valise in the other.

'Constable Eden?' he asked, and as Adam nodded, he transferred the cane to his other hand and removed his topper to reveal short, neatly barbered hair as white as bone. 'My name is Valentine,' he said. 'I am the personal physician of Mr. and Mrs. Averill — '

As soon as he heard that, Adam said urgently, 'Have you come about Meg — uh, Miss Warren? Is she all right?'

'Miss Warren is fine,' Valentine replied. 'It is *you* I have come to see.' His pale blue eyes moved fractionally to a spot beyond Adam. 'May I come in?'

Adam stepped back. 'Yes, of course. I'm sorry, my mind's been else-where . . . '

'Quite understandable, considering everything that has happened,' said Valentine, striding confidently past him into the cozy little parlor, with its table and chairs, bookcase and other odds and ends. He was, Adam thought, in his late forties, with a spare clean-shaven face turned ruddy by the cold. The eyes were somewhat close-set, the nose long and narrow, his mouth wide but thin-lipped. 'It must have been quite dreadful,' the doctor added, his voice soft and cultured, designed to put even the most anxious patient at ease.

'How may I help you, Doctor?' asked Adam.

'Yesterday afternoon I received a telegram from Mr. Averill telling me what had occurred. He was confident that Miss Warren was receiving all available care, but was somewhat concerned about you.'

171

'Me? There's no — '

'On the contrary,' interrupted Valentine. 'I believe you were soaked to the skin, after you dived into the water to save Miss Warren and then tried, gallantly but unsuccessfully, to locate and save Mr. Claydon.'

'Well, yes, but — '

'Mr. Averill asked me to come and examine you following your ordeal.'

'Well, it was hardly an ordeal for me,' Adam told him. 'I only did what anyone would do. You'd probably be better served seeing to Miss Warren, Doctor. She was the one who almost drowned, remember.'

'Even so,' Dr. Valentine said patiently, 'I have been asked to examine you, out of Mr. Averill's very genuine concern for your welfare. I believe there was some . . . friction between the two of you yesterday?'

'It was nothing more than a minor disagreement.'

'Nevertheless, Mr. Averill wishes to do all in his power to make it up to you.' Valentine set his valise on the table and opened it up. He took out a thermometer and said, 'If you will, please place this under your tongue.'

Since there was no point in trying to object, Adam thought it best to humor the man. He dutifully accepted the thermometer and stood patiently while Dr. Valentine took out a stethoscope and listened first to his chest, then to his back. At last he took the thermometer from Adam's mouth, looked at the result, then wagged it a few times before putting it back into his case.

'You're running a slight temperature,' he announced. 'And I can hear some crackling in your lungs.'

The news surprised Adam. 'Don't take this the wrong way, Doctor, but are you sure? I feel as fit today as I did yesterday.'

Dr. Valentine threw him a skeptical glance. 'It's all right, Constable,' he said, his manner a little patronizing. 'I understand. You have a responsible job and you don't want to let anyone down.

But my advice to you is to be very careful until your body fights off what I suspect is an infection of the lungs.'

'But I feel perfectly fine.'

'Of course, I may be mistaken, but I should very much doubt it,' came Valentine's terse reply. 'Based upon what I have observed, my diagnosis is a lung infection. You probably swallowed some bacteria from the water in Mare's Tail Beck. Now — roll up your right sleeve for me, will you?'

Once more he reached into the valise and withdrew a small hexagonal brown glass bottle with a cork stopper. Next came a syringe. Adam watched as he quickly filled the syringe with a pale yellow substance, and then depressed the plunger gently to expel any trapped air. 'What's that for?' he asked.

'It is what we call a caudal epidural anesthetic,' replied Valentine.

'And you want to administer that why, exactly?'

'When the effects of the infection begin to make themselves known, as they doubtless will within the next few hours, you will feel increasingly achy, you may develop a cough, a sore throat, extreme fatigue. This injection will alleviate the worst of the symptoms and enable you to carry on with your normal duties.' The doctor smiled. 'Don't worry, Constable. You won't feel a thing.'

'It's not that I'm worried about. I'd just prefer not to take anything unless I really need it.'

'You do need it.'

'I don't mean any disrespect, Doctor. I appreciate you coming here, and I appreciate Mr. Averill's concern for my welfare, but I don't want any treatment unless I need it. And honestly, I don't believe I need it.'

Dr. Valentine studied him for a long beat. At last, realizing that Adam wasn't about to change his mind, he drew a breath and said, 'Very well. But on your own head be it.'

'I'm sure I'll be — '

Before he could finish, the doctor

175

lunged forward and sent a fist crashing into his jaw. Caught completely off guard, Adam lurched backward and collided with the armchair. Valentine immediately followed, closing his fingers around Adam's throat and squeezing tightly, forcing Adam back over the arm of the chair. Adam found himself fighting for air, but Valentine wasn't about to give him any chance to get it.

'Now we'll have to do this . . . the hard way,' the doctor snarled, his voice betraying the effort he was putting into strangling his victim. 'But the . . . end result will be . . . the same. Poor . . . Constable Eden, caught and . . . succumbed to a chill after so . . . gallantly saving the life of the girl he loved. And no one will ever know . . . differently, because I will . . . sign the death certificate.'

Though confused by what the doctor was saying, Adam could piece together enough to make some sense out of it. Gerald Averill had warned him against seeing Meg. Now, apparently, he'd sent this man Valentine along to make sure of it. But what was so important about Meg that Averill would resort to murder?

Teeth clenched, Adam grabbed Valentine's wrists and tried to break his grip. For a thin man, Valentine was amazingly powerful. Lights began to pop behind Adam's eyes, and a rushing sound began to build in his ears. Then —

He tore Valentine's hands from his throat and pushed back up. The two men grappled for seconds, until Adam shoved him away. Valentine staggered and swore, while Adam, drawing air into his lungs — lungs which were anything but infected — raised his fists, Marquess of Queensberry style.

'Give it up,' he rasped, his voice hoarse. 'You're under arrest.'

Valentine only sneered at that, and with a roar came rushing back at him. He ran straight into Adam's right fist.

The doctor, if he really *was* a doctor, spun around and slammed hard against the table. His Malacca cane rolled to the edge and clattered to the floor. A moment later, he collapsed face down on the carpet, breathing heavily. Adam stood over him, shaking his hand to get some feeling back into it.

But more than anything else right then, he wanted answers. He knelt beside Valentine and turned him over. The man's eyes were open but looked vague. Adam rose again, went into the kitchen and filled a pan with water. He took it back into the living room and dashed the contents into Valentine's face. The doctor immediately sat up, gasping like a landed fish.

'You've got some explaining to do,' said Adam.

'You . . . you attacked me!' Valentine panted.

'No, I acted in self-defense,' Adam corrected him.

As full consciousness returned, Valentine eyed him slyly. 'It's your word against mine.'

Adam grabbed the other man by his lapels. 'You had better start talking,

Valentine, or whatever your name is. Why did Averill send you here to kill me?'

'Averill wanted me to check on your health,' Valentine said stubbornly. 'I was trying to do just that when you attacked me.'

'What has this got to do with Meg?' Adam grated.

'I have no idea what you're talk — '

This was taking too long. Adam let him go and stood up. Valentine watched as he opened the doctor's valise and reached inside. When his hand came back into sight, it was holding the syringe with which Valentine had been hoping to inject him. Immediately Valentine's expression turned wary.

'What are you doing with that?'

Once again Adam knelt beside him and held the syringe uncomfortably close to the other man's throat. 'Why should you care?' he replied. 'It's only . . . what did you call it? Oh yes — a 'caudal epidural anesthetic', whatever *that* is when it's at home. If I inject you with it, it will only 'alleviate the worst of your symptoms' . . . won't it?' His voice suddenly hardened. 'Or will it put you to sleep permanently?'

'You'd better put that syringe down,' warned Valentine.

'And you had better start talking,' Adam returned grimly. 'Or else.'

Valentine hesitated a moment longer. Then his eyelids fluttered and his tongue came out to wet his swollen lip. 'A-all right,' he said. 'Let me sit up and I'll . . . tell you whatever you want to know.'

Slowly Adam eased back from him and allowed the doctor to do just that. Valentine sat up carefully, keeping his eyes on the syringe, then rolled over onto his hands and knees. He reached up with one hand and Adam stiffened, then relaxed when he realized that the doctor only wanted to feel the back of his head, where it had struck the floor.

'Get on with it,' he growled.

Valentine opened his mouth to speak — and in the same movement scooped up his Malacca cane, which had rolled to a stop nearby. He brought the cane around in a quick, sharp arc and Adam felt an explosion of pain in his forehead just above his right eye as it struck. He fell sideways, desperately struggling to cling to consciousness, and Valentine leapt back to his feet and stood towering over him.

Adam looked up, his vision distorted by the stunning blow. He saw two Valentines raise the cane overhead, their clear intention being to cave in his skull. He did the only thing he could to stop it. He jammed the syringe into Valentine's leg and depressed the plunger.

Valentine screamed, and somehow the cry helped to sharpen Adam's vision again. Valentine froze, a look of absolute horror crossing his face as he realized what Adam had done. He swayed a little, his mouth opened, his arms flopped to his side and the cane slipped from his grasp. Then he fell over backwards, twitched for a moment or two, then lay still.

Adam's eyelids fluttered and he drew in a deep breath, hoping it would stave off the unconsciousness he felt sure was coming. Head hammering, he crawled on his hands and knees across to the other man. The blow had split the skin above his eye, and he could feel the blood worming down into his brow.

When he reached Valentine, he looked at the man's face; into those staring, very blue eyes. He unbuttoned the frock coat, felt for the man's heartbeat and was unable to find it. He shook a little as he realized that Valentine was dead, that he had killed him, and that he had used the very syringe with which Valentine had been planning to kill *him* to do it.

What was all this about? Try as he might, he couldn't make sense out of it. As much as anything else just then, his head ached too much for serious thinking. But if it had anything to do with Meg, if her life was in danger . . .

There came an urgent hammering at the front door.

Adam stared at it for a moment, his mind still elsewhere, the pounding in his skull making him feel increasingly nauseous. At last he grabbed the edge of the table and hauled himself to his feet, and taking a handkerchief from his pocket and trying to staunch the flow of blood from the split, he stumbled to the door.

He opened it.

And that was when he received an even greater shock.

He finally lost consciousness.

9

Meg sat on the edge of the bed and shook her head in despair. She was, as Dr. Shore had said, a fighter; and the moment Gerald had locked her in the room, she had given up trying to puzzle out his motives and just tried to concentrate on finding a way to escape.

She examined the lock briefly, not really knowing what she was looking for. Then she went in search of something with which she might force or otherwise break it. Almost immediately, her eyes found the companion set beside the fireplace. She snatched up the poker, but it was too thick to work between the lock and the frame. The dust pan, with its thinner edges, was a better bet. But after twenty minutes, all she had managed to do was splinter the frame of the door a little, and leave the lock itself untouched.

Still, the poker would serve as a weapon should she need it. And it seemed clear to her that she *would* need some means of defending herself when Gerald returned. She sensed that whatever he had in mind, he had now committed himself completely to it, and was unlikely to reconsider. But if he meant her harm, why had he been so genuinely concerned for her welfare after she had almost drowned?

That in turn made her remember the comment he had made about Adam. There could be no mistaking the implication behind it. But why did he feel the need to harm Adam, too? What had Adam ever done to him?

Feeling the need to do something, she renewed her assault on the door lock. But it was useless, unless she could find some sort of tool that was better suited to the purpose. She turned the room upside down, but found nothing. And finally, though she hated to concede defeat, she sank onto the edge of the bed and shook her head in despair.

Inside the wall, the mouse scurried

along behind the wainscoting, and it suddenly occurred to her that it was as much a prisoner here as she was.

Is that what you were trying to tell me all along, Dad? she asked silently. *Not that I should never leave, but that I would never be* permitted *to leave?*

Before she could ponder that further, she grew aware of a new sound — that of horses and harness. Her first thought was, *Adam!* And she rose and hurried to the window. Mist drifted languidly just beyond the pane, but it was thin enough for her to discern a coach following the crooked, snow-laden track toward Stormview. Hardly daring to breathe, she watched as it turned in before the house and the coachman hopped down to open the door for his passengers. Disappointment stabbed her when she saw a smartly attired man and an equally elegant woman alight. Gerald suddenly appeared to greet them, and then they all went inside, and the coachman turned his vehicle around and drove back the way he'd come.

The morning dragged on into noon. The house creaked and settled around her and was as silent as a tomb, and she was left completely alone. Once she heard the engine of the Bouton, and went back to the window in time to see Gerald driving away from the house. He was gone for perhaps an hour, and then returned.

Some time after that, the coach came rocking back down the snowy track again, and she thought the driver had come to collect his passengers. But no — he was delivering more guests, three of them this time, two men and a woman, all stylishly dressed. Once more Gerald came out to greet them and then ushered them inside, and once more the coachman turned his vehicle around and sent it back up the track and into the mist.

Meg wondered who the visitors were and whether or not they could possibly guess that their host was keeping her prisoner here in this room. Then she remembered again that it was her birthday . . . and that the very day she was born might also turn out to be the very day she died. She didn't want to think that way, but the longer she was locked up and given too much time to ponder her uncertain future, she couldn't help it.

Then, unbidden, she remembered something Gerald had said during their first meeting. *We shall do our best to ensure that your birthday is a memorable one. It is the day you come of age, Miss Warren. We will find a way to mark the occasion.*

A shiver ran through her. Was her coming of age somehow significant to him?

Desperately, she attacked the door again. The dust pan had a thin enough edge to slip between the door and the frame, but it was so narrow that she couldn't get enough leverage to really do any good.

She was still struggling to at least expose the lock when she heard the coach return for the third time, again delivering affluent-looking guests — four of them, this time, all men, whom Gerald was quick to greet and escort inside. Who were these people, and what was their purpose here? And what had happened to Adam? There had to be a way out of this room, there had to be! But try as she might, she could find no way to force the lock.

The afternoon wound tortuously on toward early evening. Once again, the coach delivered more guests. This time there were three of them. Darkness fell early, and she lit the lamp to ward off the lengthening shadows. Briefly she considered using the device to set fire to the door, but almost immediately abandoned the idea. The key to escaping from Stormview lay in secrecy; that if she were to stand any chance at all of escape, she must be long gone from here before the Averills knew it.

Evening came. Listening at the door, she heard music, and remembered the gramophone in the drawing room. There was chatter, too, and laughter, and the clink of glasses and cutlery. It sounded as if Gerald and his guests were enjoying a pleasant meal, Gerald and Leona at least seemingly indifferent to the torment they were inflicting upon her.

Grasping the poker as tightly as she could, she sat on the bed and thought, *Dad . . . if you can help me, if there's anything at all you can do to help me escape from this room . . .*

She was interrupted by the sound of the mouse behind the wainscoting. Except that this time it sounded slightly different, somehow. And it *wasn't* coming from behind the wainscoting.

There came an urgent tapping at the window.

She jumped and twisted to face the glass, and then the breath caught in her throat . . . for she could see a face outside.

Someone was there . . . thirty feet up!

★　★　★

In the dining room, Gerald suddenly stood up and excused himself, asking Leona to accompany him outside. To his guests he appeared relaxed, confident and in good spirits. But as soon as he and Leona stepped out into the foyer, his expression changed.

'Something's definitely wrong,' he said in a low voice. 'Dr. Valentine should have been here hours ago.'

Looking up at him, Leona's lips moved slowly as she repeated to herself what he had just said. Sometimes she tried so hard to understand him, it was almost pitiful. But he knew she didn't like it when he grew angry, because when he grew angry he also grew violent.

'But you went into the village,' she reminded him.

'Yes. I called on the policeman, but there was no reply. And when I asked around, no one had seen him all morning.'

'Then surely Dr. Valentine did as you asked.'

'Then where is he?' he demanded. 'When I met him from the station this morning and took him directly to the policeman's cottage, he had strict instructions to come straight here when the job was done.'

'Do you think he forgot?' she asked innocently.

He glared down at her, and she thought for a moment that he might strike her. But all he said was, 'No. But something happened that we didn't allow for. Perhaps the policeman put up a struggle, and Valentine was injured. And yet he would have let me know.'

'Unless he was too badly injured.'

He considered that. It was possible, of course, but unlikely. Dr. Valentine was cold, efficient and unbelievably tough. It was to him that Gerald had entrusted the job of bribing the headmistress, Mrs. Hewitt, to release the girl from her employment in London. Valentine had offered a substantial sum of money to make the woman do as he said — a donation to the school, and also a healthy 'consideration' to the woman . . . and still she had refused. It had been then that Dr. Valentine's true nature had shown, and it had left the headmistress terrified for her life and only too willing to accede to his request.

'Then what can we do?' asked Leona.

Gerald returned to the present. 'Without Valentine we have only twelve members here,' he said, and looked directly at her.

Her mouth dropped open, her eyes widened and she shook her head nervously. 'No,' she whispered almost tearfully. 'Please, Gerald. Don't make me see that . . . that thing again.'

'That 'thing', as you call him, is our Master,' he reminded her sternly. 'But I will not be summoning the Master tonight. However, we still need thirteen members. You will have to stand in for Valentine.'

'You're still going ahead with it, then?' she asked fearfully.

He snorted. 'Did you for one

moment ever believe that I wouldn't? Now, go upstairs and change.'

She looked surprised. 'So soon?'

He nodded. 'Without knowing for sure what has happened to Valentine, I am reluctant to wait any longer.'

Still she stood there, looking up at him, and there was something imploring in her expression. She really didn't want to do this, whether the Master was there or not.

'Go,' he said harshly. 'And Leona?'

'Yes, Gerald?'

'Don't let me down tonight,' he rasped. 'Everything I have worked for hinges on the success of tonight's ritual.'

'Yes, Gerald,' she said miserably.

'And when things are back the way they used to be,' he said, sensing that she needed an added inducement to do as she was told, 'you can have more children. Lots of them.'

It worked. Her face suddenly brightened, and she hurried away.

★ ★ ★

Meg's surprise lasted only fleetingly. Then she rushed to the window and almost tore it open. Cold air rushed into the room, but she ignored it, her attention wholly fixed on Adam; and as she grabbed him and he climbed into the room, she finally started crying, because she had convinced herself that he was dead. And yet here he was, very much alive, and he had come to save her.

'Adam . . . Adam . . . ' she sobbed, and hugged him as if she would never let him go.

'It's all right,' he said, holding her close, breathing heavily from the perilous climb he had just undertaken. 'I'm going to get you out of here.'

'But where did you come from? And what is this all about? Gerald — '

She stopped then, when she saw the tape covering the angry bruise and swelling above his right eye. 'Adam!' she breathed. 'What — ?'

'It's a long story,' he said, keeping his voice pitched low. 'I'll tell you all about

195

it when we're out of here.' He studied her closely for a moment. 'They haven't hurt you?'

'No, they just locked me in here. Adam, what's happening?'

He had been carrying a coiled rope through one arm and over his shoulder. Now he shrugged it free and turned back to the window, where he quickly tied several tight knots around the central window frame before allowing the rest of the rope to drop down into the darkness.

'You're going to need all your courage,' he said.

She stared at the rope. 'You mean — '

'It's the only way to get you out of here,' he told her. 'So long as you take your time and keep a firm grip on the rope . . . '

She started breathing rapidly just at the thought of what lay ahead for her — a slow descent into cold misty darkness, with the chance of slipping, or being discovered at any moment.

'Hand over hand and you'll soon

reach the ground,' he said. 'Trust me — coming up was the hard part, and I didn't even have a rope to help me. I had to climb up through all that ivy.'

She continued to stare at the rope, knowing she had no choice if she wanted to escape.

From somewhere up above, a bell began tolling. *The* bell.

He looked at her. 'Quickly now,' he said. And when she hesitated he added, 'I'll look after you.'

Without realizing it, he had said exactly the same thing he'd said that day when they had decided to explore Stormview; and in a way she could never hope to explain, that simple statement gave her the confidence she needed.

Then the bell stopped.

'Go,' he hissed.

She started for the window. But they'd left it too late; for even now, they heard a key turning in the lock.

Adam looked around, spotted the poker on the counterpane, and went to snatch it up just as the door opened and Gerald stood there, wearing a tar-black monk's habit . . . and carrying a revolver in his hand.

His surprise at seeing Adam there lasted only a moment. Then he jabbed the gun in Adam's direction, and Adam froze. Behind Gerald, his guests were gathered in the hallway, and they too were wearing habits and cowls, as was a pale-faced Leona.

'Well,' said Gerald after a long pause. 'I imagine your presence here explains Dr. Valentine's continued absence.'

Adam went back to stand beside Meg. 'It's not too late to call this off, you know.'

Gerald smiled coolly. 'It is,' he countered. 'It's far too late.' Stepping to one side, he turned his head and snapped to his followers, 'Take them to the tower!'

The male guests entered the room. Adam braced himself to fight them, but he never stood a chance; there were simply too many of them. There was a brief, brave struggle, but then they had him, and Meg; and although she struggled every step of the way, they were slowly but surely dragged from the room and then pushed and shoved along the hallway, around the corner, through the doorless aperture and up the thirteen steps to the ice-cold tower.

The room had been lit with candles, a hundred or perhaps two hundred of them, standing in ranks like wax soldiers on every flat surface. Thin wisps of noxious black smoke trickled from every flame up to the roof, and the shadows they made wavered to and fro with every stray breeze.

Finding herself back in this room with its blasphemous cross, sheathed knife and pentagram, Meg felt that there was no longer even the faintest hope that they might escape. She asked desperately, 'Why are you doing this?'

Gerald's eyes found hers. 'Your father,' he said simply.

Silence filled the room.

'My father's dead,' she said after a

moment. 'He committed suicide.'

Gerald shook his head. 'Your father didn't commit suicide, Miss Warren,' he replied. 'We killed him.'

For Meg, it felt as if the floor shifted beneath her, and she felt Adam take her arm to stop her from falling altogether.

'That is to say, the members of our sect at the time killed him,' Gerald clarified. Seeing her disbelief, he added, 'Oh, we didn't do it intentionally, though I confess we would have eventually. He gave us no choice.'

'What do you mean?' asked Adam. He knew exactly what Gerald meant, but he was trying to stall the man and give himself time to work out how he might yet save them from the fate that now seemed inevitable.

Fortunately, Gerald was happy to indulge him. 'The dark forces, as you ill-informed outsiders call them, have been very good to us,' he said. 'We have embraced all that is unholy and served our Master well. Obedience to his every wish, the sacrifice of blood as a means to show him our loyalty . . . and in return, he has helped us all in our endeavors. How do you think my father amassed such a fortune? He was a businessman, true, but he was not an especially gifted one. But our Master rewards his most faithful followers, and he has done so for each and every one of us.

'But secluded though we are here at Stormview, our . . . activities were sometimes witnessed by others — people who had no business here. Poachers, sometimes the plain curious, and even simple-minded thrill-seekers. And through them, rumors began to circulate as to what we did here.

'Of course, most people dismissed it all as idle gossip. Denial and disbelief are the things we have always relied upon to keep our secrecy. What people find too distressing, too frightening, too *incredible* . . . they choose simply to dismiss.

'I believe your father was like that, Miss Warren, to begin with. But when the stories persisted, he decided to make some investigations of his own.

'And so he began to spy upon us, and he did so very successfully, for it was a long time before we realized that he was different to the rest; that he would not dismiss the rumors until he had proved to himself that they were groundless.' He smiled coldly. 'What follows must of course be conjecture, for we do not know exactly what happened next, though it is easy enough to guess. He came out here under cover of darkness one night and saw, or heard, one of our rituals. It confirmed his suspicions, that we did indeed worship the one true Master. And from that, it followed that all the rumors of blood sacrifice must also be true. He did not see us as the villagers did, as witches, or warlocks, or Satanists. He saw us as murderers, and in the eyes of the law — the law he was so pitifully proud to uphold — we must pay.

'But before he could entertain any notions of arresting us, he had to have proof. And so one night he broke into Stormview in search of evidence he might use to convince his superiors to issue an arrest warrant. He searched high and low until he found the room in which you now find yourself, Miss Warren. And here, with all the trappings of the forbidden religion we have chosen to follow, he found the very thing he could use against us — the *Netherbane Codex*.'

Meg shook her head, struggling to comprehend everything she was being told. 'What — ?'

'It is a book,' snapped Gerald. 'Though not just any book. It was written in the sixteenth century, shortly before Pope Innocent VIII issued his *Summis desiderantes affectibus*, the document which recognized witchcraft as a threat to Christendom and gave approval for his emissaries to hound, persecute, torture and execute any and all of its practitioners. It is a book of spells, one of the most powerful of its kind, and my father paid a fortune to possess the one copy known to have survived the purge.

'The spells contained within its pages are many and varied. It had taken many scholars many lifetimes to translate them from the original secret codes. The knowledge within them was ours to do with as we chose . . . until your father stole the book away from us.

'But he did not manage to leave as silently as he had arrived. One of the servants saw him escaping with the *Codex* under his arm. The alarm was raised, and my father and the forebears of the people you now see before you all gave chase.

'Your father gave a good account of himself, Miss Warren. Perhaps fear gave him a fleetness of foot he would not otherwise have possessed. But we eventually ran him to ground on Serenity Bridge.'

Meg felt a tremble race through her. She was on the verge of learning a great truth and wasn't at all sure she could take it.

'There was just one problem,' Gerald continued. 'By the time we caught him, he was no longer in possession of the *Netherbane Codex*. Somewhere along the way he had stopped and hidden it, perhaps as insurance should we catch him, as indeed we did.

'My father was furious, as well he might be. If the *Netherbane Codex* was priceless, then the information it contained was even more so. There and then your father was taken by the arms, forced to his knees and beaten until he confessed the whereabouts of the book.'

'Except,' Adam interrupted softly, 'he never confessed.'

'He never confessed,' admitted Gerald. 'Which was very foolish, for we Averills have never been given to mercy, and were quite prepared to punish him, his wife . . . and indeed you, Miss Warren, to loosen his tongue.

'When my father told him as much, he renewed his struggles against those men who held him; and battered and beaten though he was, this time he was able to free himself from their grasp. He tried to make another break for freedom, but the men who had been charged with holding him gave chase, and there was a struggle, during which your father went over the bridge and into the beck.

'By the time they managed to fish him from the water, it was too late. He had struck his head on a rock that lay just beneath the surface and, unconscious, had drowned. So we had lost the book, and the only man who could have told us where it was hidden.

'My father had Constable Warren thrown back into the river, and thereafter circulated the story that he had in a fit of depression taken his own life. It was a lie that not even the county coroner thought to question. As for the Codex, my father was not unduly worried at first. He felt that there were only so many hiding places you father could have chosen. After all, he was fleeing for his very life. He did not have the time to choose the best place, only the most expedient one. He was confident that we would find the *Codex* with a little diligent searching.'

His eyes suddenly went flat. 'We did not.'

Meg was hardly listening to him now. She was thinking of her father and how he had really died in the line of duty, a brave man who had tried to do a good thing and been thwarted by the evil men and women who had hounded him. And she thought she understood something else, too — the true meaning of the cryptic message he had tried to impart to her. He had not been saying *never leave*. He had been trying to tell her to *leave* because of the *Netherbane Codex*!

She also remembered the strange visit her mother had received shortly after her father's death. She had never quite understood why Vincent Averill had come to extend his sympathies. He hadn't known her father, and rarely if ever showed himself in the village. But suddenly she understood. Unable to find the book of spells by which he and this . . . this sect had set such store, he had tried to question her mother to see if he had any particularly favorite places he knew or liked to visit; places where he might possibly have hidden the book.

Her mother had been unable to help, of course, but she must have been unnerved by Averill's visit, because very shortly after that she had moved them to London to live with her sister, Meg's Aunt Rachel. And the poor woman had lived in fear after that; and the dread she had always exhibited, and which Meg had misconstrued, had been that one of Vincent Averill's followers would find them.

But further thought was stopped as Gerald continued his story. 'My father died a broken man,' he said, speaking with a bitter edge now. 'He felt that by his failure to retrieve the *Netherbane Codex*, he had let our Master down and let down our sect. There was nothing he could do to bring it back where it belonged. He turned the estate upside down, and still it eluded him. And he took the shame of that, the guilt of his failure, with him to the grave.

'That was when it became *my* life's work to reclaim the *Codex*. I read every arcane manuscript I could lay my hands on, until I found the answer — to bring your father back from the afterlife and force him to tell me what he had done with it.'

Meg's hazel-gray eyes saucered. 'You're insane!' she breathed, but he only shook his head, and a triumphant smile touched his mouth.

'No, not insane. Anything but insane. I discovered the spell, you see. The incantation that would wrench him from his rest and compel him to answer my questions. I have learned the spell by heart — I could probably recite it in my sleep, for it has become an obsession with me. But I had to learn something else besides. I had to learn to be patient, for the spell required the blood of your father's blood; that the child of the man I intended to resurrect attain his or her twenty-first year, and that he or she still be of untouched purity.'

His smile now turned to one of contempt. 'Well, you are now twenty-one, and by your own admission you are sinless and chaste. And with the spilling of your blood this night, and the tolling of that bell, your father will be summoned and can do nothing but reveal where he hid the *Codex*.'

She shook her head again, and he raised one eyebrow.

'You think I can't do it?' he asked. 'You think it impossible to raise the dead, or summon spirits? Then you are even more naive than I thought, for both things are possible. I have seen as much with my own eyes. I have performed such rites. But you must take my word for it, Miss Warren . . . for by the time your father is summoned, you will be dead.'

Adam stepped forward. 'You might not be insane, Averill, but you're most certainly deluded if you believe all the gibberish you've just spouted. You're in trouble enough as it is, man, without making it any worse! Now listen to me — '

Gerald stepped forward and lashed out with a vicious backhand blow that sent Adam stumbling. As he righted himself and swiped blood from his lip, Gerald turned his attention back to Meg. 'Prepare her,' he said without taking his eyes from hers.

Two male members of the sect came forward. Meg retreated until she felt the altar at the small of her back and knew she could go no further. Desperately she looked from left to right; and then, reaching behind her, she snatched up the knife and threw it, sheath and all, at the nearest of her would-be assailants.

The man dodged aside and the weapon sailed past him to land with a clatter against the tile floor. But it provided a distraction, and Adam seized it. With a frantic yell of 'Run!', he threw himself at the second man.

His momentum sent them both crashing into the wall. The man tried to bring his arms up to defend himself, but his movements were restricted by the heavy gown he wore. Before he could do so, Adam hit him on the jaw and the man spilled over.

By then Meg was dashing to the door, but as quick as she was, she wasn't quick enough for Gerald. Like a blur, he reached out and grabbed a handful of her hair.

She came up short, with a wince and a groan. Then Gerald was behind her, one arm hooked around her throat, even as Adam prepared to tackle another of the sect members who had moved swiftly to block his way.

'Eden!' Gerald bellowed, and the name echoed around the room.

Adam saw Meg in his grasp and bitterly allowed his hands drop to his sides.

Gerald sneered. 'You can't get away, either of you,' he said. 'But I appreciate that you had to try.' The smile vanished abruptly and he shoved Meg back toward the altar. 'Prepare her,' he said again. 'And as for you, Constable . . . ' He took the gun from the folds of his habit and tossed it to the man who had dodged the thrown knife. 'Kill him,' he said dispassionately.

The man caught the weapon and took one step toward Adam when, without warning, the tower room door slammed open behind Gerald and a voice yelled, 'Leave him alone! Leave them both alone, damn you!'

Before anyone could react, the newcomer grabbed Gerald from behind and locked his big hands to either side of Gerald's skull.

Leona screamed.

'Stop, all of you!' cried the newcomer. 'Or so help me, one twist and I'll break his neck!'

Meg looked at the speaker and felt certain that she would faint.

For the man who had just made such a dramatic entrance was John Claydon!

10

John looked across the room at Adam. 'Get her out of here and to safety!' he said.

There was no surprise in Adam's expression as he looked at the man Meg had believed dead. He only snatched the revolver from the man who had intended to kill him and then hurried across the floor to take Meg by one arm and propel her toward the door. With every step she took, her eyes remained fixed upon John.

'What about you?' Adam asked when he was close enough.

John still held Averill's head in a vise-like grip, and she knew that if he had to, he would indeed kill Gerald with one quick wrench.

'I'll be along,' he said. 'Now get her away from here!'

They went past him and side by side

hurried along the cold corridor with the breath misting before their faces. Meg heard herself whisper, 'I don't understand. John — he died.'

'That's what he wanted everyone to believe,' Adam answered, keeping them moving down the staircase to the foyer. 'It was safer for him that way.'

She looked at him. 'You knew?'

'Not at first,' he said. 'It's a long story.'

'Tell me.'

They came off the staircase and crossed the foyer. Without stopping, he said, 'John has been with the Averills for years. At first he was ignorant of what the family was up to. By the time he found out, he was too scared to report them and feared that if he were to try and leave, they would find him and kill him to protect their secret. So he tried to convince himself that the Averills and their cronies were just rich people indulging themselves, a bit like old society, the Hellfire Club. And that's what he kept telling himself, until he learned what the Averills had in store for you. Then . . .'

But before he could finish, there came an outburst of yelling from above, in the midst of which was a cry of pain that froze Meg's blood in her veins. She looked directly into Adam's face. His expression was grim.

'They got him,' he said softly. And then: 'Run!'

Adam tore open the door and they burst out into the full force of a fresh storm. At once they were bombarded by a million freezing pellets of snow and surrounded by the swirling mass, Meg's sense of direction completely deserting her. If it hadn't been for Adam's firm grip on her wrist, she wouldn't have known where she was going.

They ran on through the darkness, slipping and sliding. It took only seconds for the biting wind to make itself felt, plastering snow against their chilled skin, caking it over their fluttering eyelashes. Meg slipped and

216

would have fallen but for Adam's support. Her flesh numbed and her expression grew immobile as the cold robbed it of all sensation.

Dimly above the roar of the wind, she heard voices behind them raised in anger and excitement. She risked a look over one shoulder, saw that the door to the great, misshapen house hung open, and in the light spilling out from the foyer Averill and his followers could be seen, pouring down the stone steps in a tide, hurrying in pursuit.

She thought suddenly that they were never going to outrun them; that Gerald and his sect must inevitably run them to ground, just as old Vincent Averill and his followers had chased her father all those years before.

But the thought of her father, of his courage and dedication to the villagers he had sworn to protect, suddenly filled her with new resolve. As cold as she was, as harsh the conditions and the terrain, they *must* outrun their pursuers. The alternative was unthinkable.

'Damn!'

She looked at Adam. He had slipped, and as he regained his balance, dropped Gerald's revolver. There was no time to retrieve it — all they could do was keep moving.

All at once they were climbing the slope toward the trees, the same slope they had climbed all those years before, and each of them was fighting for breath and pushing on when their every muscle begged for them to stop.

At last they were in among the trees, and they were some protection, though not much, from the snowstorm. Meg felt the breath rasping in her throat, heard the pulsing of blood in her ears, felt the hammering of her heart against her ribs. Still Adam dragged her on, and still she fought against every urge to stop and catch her second wind, and did her best to keep up with him.

'Can . . . can we hide?' she asked.

He looked down at her. 'There's nowhere they won't find us,' he replied. But he saw how badly she was struggling now, and abruptly came to a halt. Facing her, he put his hands on her shoulders and said, 'Just rest a moment and get your breath back.'

'We can't afford — '

'We can't afford *not* to,' he interrupted. 'If we can just get to Serenity Bridge . . . '

While he glanced off in that direction, she said, 'Tell me . . . about John. When did you . . . find out he was . . . still alive?'

'This morning,' he replied. 'And I had the shock of my life when . . . when he turned up on my doorstep.'

'I don't really understand any of this,' she said in a small voice.

'It was only when John overhead what the Averills had in mind for you that he realized he could delude himself no longer,' Adam explained quickly. 'He could go along with it and be a party to murder, or he could do what he should have done all those years ago when your father died at the hands of Vincent Averill's men.'

'He chose to speak out?'

Adam nodded. 'As he explained it, he was on his way to see me and make a full confession when the coach crashed into the water. He hit the water hard and lost consciousness. When he came to, his first instinct was to save you — until he saw me coming along. Then he realized that he might be safer if everyone believed he was dead. So he hid . . . and this morning he finally came to my cottage and told me everything. I'd have come sooner, but I had some troubles of my own.' He touched the bump on his forehead. 'I was unconscious for most of the day.'

Before he could say more, they heard someone yelling in the distance, and Adam's face suddenly set hard. 'We'd better push on,' he said.

He took her hand, and his touch was like a balm to her. Heedless of her exhaustion, of the cold and damp and the shocks she had received this day and night, she continued on, doing her best to keep up with him.

'I never believed that your father killed himself,' he said as the trees passed them in a blur. 'Even when I was a lad, I couldn't believe it. But now we know the truth. I only hope — '

Just then the forest fell behind them, and once again they were exposed to the full force of the storm. The wind shoved against them, slowing their progress, and Adam turned, drew Meg into his embrace and almost carried her on.

'What do you hope?' Meg called, her words torn away by the wind. In a sudden break in the snow, she saw Serenity Bridge up ahead and shuddered. The span had always held painful memories for her. Now that she knew the truth about her father, the pain of his loss stabbed at her even deeper. But even as they stepped onto the bridge's thick timbers, she felt Adam's hands give her a squeeze of encouragement. 'That — '

Just then, there came a crash of sound so loud she heard it plainly above the howl of the wind. At almost the same moment she felt Adam twitch, and when she looked at him his face was screwed up in pain.

She stared at him. 'Adam — ?'

'Keep going!' he grated.

He tried to push her forward, for his own pace was flagging, and she realized with a tug of fear that the sound she had heard had been a gunshot . . . and that the bullet had found Adam as its target.

Even as she thought it, he stumbled and dropped to one knee, his right arm wrapped around his body so that he could clasp his limp left arm close. Through the snow she saw something red and slick on his sleeve, and then he folded forward at the waist with the pain of the wound.

'Adam!'

'Go!' he cried.

The yelling was getting closer now. Whoever had fired the weapon — almost certainly Gerald, having retrieved his revolver — knew he'd scored a hit. She spared a glance at the lane leading back into the trees, then turned her eyes once more to Adam, knowing that she loved this man in the way he had always loved her, and that no one was going to take him away from her, not if she could help it.

Unbidden, she suddenly thought back to that day of their childhood, when they had fled from Stormview, convinced that all the demons of hell were on their heels. She remembered how she had stumbled and twisted her ankle, how the other children had kept running . . . and how Adam had stayed with her, and planted himself between her and their pursuers, be they real or imaginary . . . how he had stood his ground to protect her.

Even as the yells of their all-too-real pursuers now grew closer, she realized she could do no less for Adam now. It was foolish, she knew — what could she hope to do, save deliver herself back into their hands? And yet . . .

She could see them now, Gerald,

Leona and the others, the cowls and shoulders of their robes encrusted with snow. And she saw, too, the revolver in Gerald's hand, and still she put herself between them and Adam. They saw her do this, and slowing, Gerald said something to his companions, who were fanned out to either side of him, and they laughed.

They stepped onto the bridge and kept coming. Meg watched them through eyes that flickered constantly as snow blew into her face. Behind her, Adam staggered back to his feet and put his good hand on her shoulder. 'Run, girl!' he said.

But if running meant leaving Adam behind, then she would *not* run.

No more than fifty feet separated them now from Gerald and his sect. Gerald raised the revolver again, but Meg knew he would not shoot — not if he wished to keep her alive for his dreadful ritual.

'You've given us some sport we would rather have avoided,' he said, lifting his voice to be heard above the moan of the wind. 'But no matter. You're ours again, now.'

'Let it go, Averill,' managed Adam. 'There's nothing to be gained by harming Meg.'

'On the contrary,' said Averill. 'There is everything to gain. The *Netherbane Codex* — '

'It's gone, Averill. It was destroyed years ago.'

Gerald came to a halt, as did his companions. 'You're lying,' he said.

Adam shook his head. 'Constable Warren hid the book, right enough,' he replied. 'But with your father on his heels, he didn't have time to hide it as well as he would have liked. It was found almost immediately . . . by John Claydon.'

Again, Gerald said, 'You're lying.' But he no longer sounded as sure of himself as he had just moments before.

'While your father was chasing Constable Warren, John came out after *him*. He found the book that your father had overlooked in his haste to catch up with Meg's father, and would have given it back to him had he not seen you people beat and then kill the constable. Then, terrified for his own life, he took the book back to his quarters with him. When he looked at it, and saw by as much as he could understand of its writing and illustrations exactly what it was, and decided to destroy it.' He paused as another wave of pain coursed through his wounded arm. 'He did,' he said at last. 'He burned it to ashes.'

Gerald's eyes were large in his face. 'No!'

Adam nodded. 'Yes, Averill. You and your father spent all those years searching for a book you were never going to find again. The *Netherbane Codex* was destroyed years ago — and good riddance to it.'

A murmur ran through the sect members. This information, if true, changed everything. Without the book, their power and all the rewards they felt it would bring them was greatly diminished.

'I don't believe you,' said Gerald.

'I don't care whether you believe me or not,' said Adam. 'It's the truth.'

Gerald was silent for a long time, as the blizzard swept around them. Adam sagged a little, and instinctively Meg reached to steady him. She looked up into his face, her eyes asking the question. He nodded.

'That was something else John told me,' he said quietly. 'When he realized the evil that book held, he couldn't destroy it quickly enough.'

'Take them!' Gerald shouted suddenly. 'We'll question him further back at Stormview, and he'll tell us the truth if he wants to spare the girl any pain!'

Leona said, 'And what if he *is* telling the truth? What then, Gerald?'

'There must be another copy of the book somewhere in the world! I'll continue to search until I've found it!'

Adam said softly, 'Meg, please. Get away from h — '

But by then it was too late. Gerald's followers were hurrying forward, hands outstretched to grab them and drag them back to the twisted, misshapen house.

'I love you, Adam,' she said.

'I love you,' he replied. 'I always have.'

Before she could respond to that, however, someone behind them called out, 'Stop where you are, all of you! Stop, in the name of the law!'

And then, seemingly out of nowhere, a dozen uniformed policemen brandishing bull's-eye lanterns against the darkness of the night ran past them across the bridge. Gerald and the others, seeing them coming, froze momentarily, then quickly turned to run, but the policemen were upon the majority before they managed to get ten paces. The remainder, including Gerald, made it into the trees, but five or six policemen sprinted after them. There was more yelling, a couple of wild gunshots, and then out of the storm the policemen reappeared, shoving a now-disarmed Gerald, Leona and the remaining sect members ahead of them.

When all the prisoners were herded together and under careful watch, a short, chubby man in a uniform that carried the stripes of an inspector broke away from the group and approached them. As he did so, he noted Adam's wound as if for the first time.

'Are you all right, lad?' he asked. He was in his early fifties, with dark, sharp eyes and an impressive handlebar moustache. He looked pale, but Meg got the feeling it was more through shock at what he had so recently seen and overheard than anything to do with the bitterness of the weather.

'I'm . . . all right, sir,' Adam husked through clenched teeth.

'Well, we'll soon get that scratch seen to,' said the inspector, as if the wound were just a trifle. And then, with a polite salute to Meg: 'Inspector Burridge, ma'am, Devon County Constabulary. Miss Warren, is it?'

Not trusting herself to speak, Meg only nodded.

'I remember your father, Miss Warren,' said the inspector. 'He was a good man and a fine officer. Had it not been for your involvement in this affair, I confess I would have screwed up the telegram I received from young Eden here and given him a right dressing down for wasting my time. Witches and warlocks, indeed! And yet . . . ' His expression sobered. 'And yet it seems he was onto something after all,' he finished quietly.

'If you don't . . . mind me saying so, sir,' said Adam, 'you cut it awfully fine, turning up.'

'Oh, we were here in plenty of time, just as you asked us to be,' replied the inspector, 'but you were nowhere to be found. We were just about to push on to Stormview when you two came into sight. Only a fool could fail to notice that you were running for your lives, so I took the decision to hold back and see what happened next.'

'Well, you saw,' said Meg, her voice

still a little unsteady from their brush with death. 'Now what?'

Burridge's eyes grew flinty as they settled on the prisoners, all of whom were staring back at him balefully, a few — Gerald included — telling the watching officers what a mistake they were making in treating them this way, and how the Devon County Constabulary would be hearing from their solicitors.

'These are important people, aren't they?' he said. 'Powerful people.'

'Yes, sir,' said Adam.

'And because of that, because of who they know, they think they'll doubtless walk free from any charges I bring against them.'

'Yes, sir,' Adam repeated.

'Well, this might be 1906,' said Burridge, 'but in the eyes of the law, witchcraft is still a very serious crime. Add to that a clear case of abduction, attempted murder — '

' — and actual murder, sir,' Adam interrupted grimly. When Burridge looked back at him, Adam said, 'Averill's sect was complicit in the murder of Meg's father, sir — he confessed that to us himself. And subsequently they spread the rumor that Constable Warren had committed suicide. I believe you'll also find the body of John Claydon up at the house. They killed him barely twenty minutes ago.'

'In that case,' said Burridge, and his voice was soft now, and all the more dangerous because of it, 'I will personally see to it that their power and influence count for nothing when this comes to trial. I will make my concerns known to the Home Secretary, and he will ensure that Averill and his cronies are shown no special favors.'

'Can we guarantee that?' asked Meg.

'When this all comes out,' Burridge replied, and he smiled at last, albeit grimly, 'I think the good old British public will make sure the Home Secretary sees that justice is served. Now, if you'll excuse me, Miss Warren, I have to get this lot back to Exeter, and charged.

We have vehicles back along the road a ways — I'll have someone run you both back into Pendarren, where Dr. Shore can check you both over — and stop you bleeding all over your uniform, young Eden.' So saying, he turned and went back to the waiting prisoners and their grim-looking guards.

Adam reached his good arm around Meg's shoulders and held her tightly. 'I know it's a silly question,' he said, 'but . . . are you all right?'

She looked up at him. 'I will be,' she replied softly. 'But I never want to see Stormview again.'

He nodded. 'I guessed that.' He hesitated, then said, 'Do you think you'll go back to London?'

'I'd like to,' she replied. 'I miss St Nicholas's, and the children there. And even if I can't go back to Nicholas's, I'm sure there must be other schools that take in underprivileged children and give them a chance in life.' She shivered. 'I'd miss you, though, Adam. I'd miss you terribly.'

He shook his head. 'You won't have to. I'll be coming with you, if you'll have me.'

Her eyes searched his face. 'What do you mean?'

'It means I lost you once. I'm not about to lose you again. I'll follow you to the ends of the earth, if I have to.'

'But your job . . . '

'They need policemen in London, too, I believe.'

'Well, of course they do. But — '

'Then I'm sure a transfer to the Metropolitan Police District can be arranged.'

Tears moved in her eyes. 'You'd do that for me?'

'That and more,' he replied.

'Then a spell *was* cast tonight,' she whispered as they turned their steps away from Stormview, away from Serenity Bridge, and back toward the police van, and Pendarren, and safety.

'And trust me,' he whispered, bending to kiss her hair, 'it's one spell that will *never* be broken.'